VINCE CHURCHILL

PREY FOR THE DAMNED

PREY FOR THE DAMNED

by

Vince Churchill

2nd Edition Trade Paperback 2025
1st Edition 2022

All Rights Reserved

CHURCHILL ENTERTAINMENT

Churchill Entertainment

6600 S. 6th St. Frontage Rd. E.

Springfield, Illinois USA 62712

Edited by Monica O'Rourke
Cover by Bailey Hunter - Title Lettering by Joel Andrade
Inset Design by Bailey Hunter

ISBN: 978-1-965426-13-5

Other Titles
by Vince Churchill

HYDE

GOODNIGHT, MY SWEET

MIDNIGHT ETERNAL

RUN! (a children's book)

SEVEN

THE DEAD SHALL INHERIT THE EARTH

DEATH AND OTHER CONSEQUENCES
(a grim collection)

THE BLACKEST HEART

PANDORA

THE BUTCHER BRIDE

TABLE OF CONTENTS

Satisfaction Guaranteed............................7

A Day at the Beach 16

You Can't Go Home Again........................23

The Admiration of Scars........................29

How Legends Are Born, Heroes Unmade 34

The New King of the Streets 54

Pearls before Swine............................56

Young and Old Alike 64

Roll Call....................................73

The Last Sunset Dunes........................83

Sand Worms................................93

Home Is Where the Horror Is.................. 103

Pulling the Wings off Flies 112

Fangs for the Memories........................120

A Field of Dead Roses........................129

Postmortem 143

Have You Checked the Children? 150

The Last Boy Scout.......................... 170

California-Style BBQ..........................180

High School Reunion..........................189

The Final Pieces of the Puzzle.................. 197

The Beginning of the End 205

When the Ocean Swallows the Sun...............208

Working on the Chain, Gang 227

And a Soggy Cherry on Top 231

1
SATISFACTION GUARANTEED

Cloaked in the alley's gloom, Cheyenne squatted and reached into her oversized lemon-colored purse. Ignoring the departing footsteps of her latest customer, she retrieved a shiny metal flask and took a healthy swig. She swished the liquid around her mouth, enjoying the mild tingling sensation. Spitting out the mouthwash, she parted ways with the salty aftermath of another satisfied john, swiping her mouth and chin with a moist baby wipe. Happy endings were worth extra bucks per blowjob, and that translated into a semester's worth of gas for her scooter.

She reapplied her lipstick using a lighted compact and then checked the time on her phone. She had an hour before her weekly hookup with Mr. Winters at Italy's Best, a neighborhood Italian place. A seventy-something widower, Mr. Winter always reserved the cozy couple's booth at the back of the restaurant. In the romantic lighting, she would slide into the booth next to him, and they would chat about the events of the day. He would sip his wine while she snuggled against him. A well-rehearsed routine. She casually slipped a hand under the table, deftly undid his belt and zipper, and gave him an expert hand job. Prior to their first session, he'd shared that his beloved wife,

Madeline, had performed the duty during their weekly visits to the restaurant. Cancer had taken her life almost a decade ago, but several months back he swore his beloved had come to him in a dream and told him it was okay for him to recreate their decadent dates at the neighborhood's favorite eating spot.

Cheyenne enjoyed making the elderly man feel good, and he always slipped her a crisp $50 bill for the brief encounter. He'd smile, thank her for her time, and pronounce he looked forward to seeing her the next week. Cheyenne knew their weekly date was an open secret among the staff, but no one ever gave either of them a judgmental or disapproving look. Mr. Winter was the respected, retired personal tailor of the small-time local mob. Cheyenne Benjamin was the former high school prom queen and valedictorian left to struggle through her final year of college after the death of her parents in a tragic mall shooting spree.

Cheyenne straightened her blouse and skirt before walking the opposite direction from her trick. She maneuvered through the dark alley like a stray cat, comfortable in the shadows. She knew the alleys of her Pacific Grove beach community like the back of her hand, just one of the many great lessons she'd learned running the streets with the Waves. The clinging smells and gathering trash were just natural parts of her environment, like dirty cops or a woman's period.

A few steps from the Pacific Avenue sidewalk, she heard a noise. She froze. She couldn't place the sound but recognized it as odd, unnatural. Still cloaked in shadows, she listened. Faint dialogue pierced the quiet. She couldn't make out the words, but instinct told her to stay out of sight.

It was a shakedown. A hitter from one of the local silk purses collecting a late payment from some Joe in the darkness of her alley as it continued across the street. She eased her hand into her purse and withdrew her glasses. She'd been told they didn't diminish her attractiveness, but her ego wouldn't accept the truth. Her budget couldn't afford contacts until she finished school and landed a good job.

She looked across the street, beyond the rear of the furniture store delivery van. A pair of bright yellow lights illuminated the loading dock halfway down the alley, but the action was happening closer to the street end. She struggled with her street-smart inner voice. It barked at her to drop her eyes and back away. This was none of her business, and once evening turned into night, downtown Pacific Grove became a whole different kind of workplace. A murder involving a teenage couple returning home from a movie date happened a couple of nights ago. Details had been sketchy, but rumors were the deaths had been described by cops as gruesome and unnatural. Neighborhoods had closed ranks just a bit more as police continued to investigate. Cheyenne was relieved there'd been no mention of gang violence. She'd heard the Waves were having a tough enough time dealing with the political volleyball of "Colors for Careers" gang dissolution program.

The scene across the way was too mesmerizing in its break from reality for her not to watch.

Two men and a woman were half in and out of the shadows. Cheyenne recognized one of the men and would have even without the aqua and black leather vest displaying his gang affiliation. The man pinned to the furniture store brick wall was Stallion, a member of the Waves, Pacific Grove's white-hat street gang. The muscular, blond-maned gang member towered over the man who, with one hand, had the former seventeen-and-under California light-heavyweight Golden Gloves boxing champion held in check. Stallion struggled, both large hands unable to pry the smaller man's hand from his throat. The muscles in his arm flexed and bulged with his effort to free himself. In high school, those impressive arms had circled the shoulders and waists of countless drooling female students. Cheyenne might have been among the seduced, but his ego was even bigger than his biceps. Plus, she'd always thought Bam's arms were bigger. She'd always favored the Waves' leader, Wallace Thornton, known as Breeze. He was better looking, wasn't conceited, and had the best set of abs in Southern California. He'd also been pretty funny, in a sneaky, subtle way.

Looking on was Stallion's flavor of the month, a pretty dropout named Cassie. No, Sissy. Something like that. Flame-red hair flowed to her shoulder blades, and shapely legs sprouted from under a plaid miniskirt she'd kept around to use with her sexy schoolgirl Halloween costume. Her perky, braless breasts sat under a thin white sweater. She still wore the same stoplight red lipstick she'd used as a cheerleader half a decade ago. Cheyenne had heard a rumor the woman had a brief career as a professional wrestler. Seemed a perfect fit for the slutty attention whore.

The woman pleaded with the aggressor to stop, fear filling her voice. The man appeared completely focused on Stallion's helplessness. Cheyenne couldn't help focusing on the smaller man, her mind unable to accept what was happening.

Timothy Doleman was the manager down at Style's Deli and Bakery. He was a quiet guy, nice enough. He was whip thin with a pasty complexion, but he never seemed weak or sickly. She couldn't remember seeing him with a girl, not even back in high school, but he didn't put out a creepy loner vibe. She'd once called him Tim, but he'd pushed his glasses back up his beak-like nose and announced his name was Timothy, after his great-grandfather. He hadn't seemed offended, and he wasn't rude, just proud of who he was. He hadn't been a jock in school, and as far as she knew, he hadn't taken up any sports since. But now he was displaying a stunning feat of strength. She didn't know how much Stallion weighed, but it was well beyond what Timothy should have been able to lift with both hands, much less one.

What she saw was insane. As was Timothy's other hand—if it could still be described as such. His fingers had the appearance of a spider's legs, too long to be human. Even at this distance, she could see boney knots where the joints should have been, and his nails ended in wicked, bird-of-prey talons.

When Cheyenne's flight instincts barked at her nervous system, she listened. But even as her body flinched to turn and run, the scene across the way changed. It snared her attention like a hangman's noose, drawing her out of the alley's dark cloak.

Stallion's struggles became more frantic, and Cheyenne saw Timothy's fingers burrowing into the flesh of the gang member's throat. Sissy screamed at the savage invasion. As casual as swatting a gnat, Timothy backhanded the redhead across the face, tossing the young woman into the middle of Pacific Avenue like an empty beer can. Sissy's body flopped and rolled with sickening crunches. Cheyenne flinched, thinking the woman's head had struck the road. But that wasn't right.

11

Mesmerized by the mayhem, Cheyenne stepped to the edge of the street.

Sissy lay in a heap. Stomach down, her stiletto heels pointed toward the dark sky. So did her bloody, misshapen face. The blow had caved in her cheekbone and the side of her skull. Her head sat backward on her broken neck like a mistreated doll. Her death stare cursed the universe for its cruelty.

The sudden screech of car brakes broke the spell. Men shouted as they spilled from the vehicle, questioning and threatening in profanity-filled tirades.

Cheyenne moved without thinking, dropping to a knee beside Sissy. The dead girl's eye bulged obscenely, threatening to burst from its socket. Cheyenne's stomach flipped and twisted, her early dinner of a chili cheese dog and French fries gushing from her mouth. Guts still convulsing, more screaming filled the air.

From all fours, Cheyenne looked through her dark bangs at the horror show across the street. Stallion was on the ground, clutching at his ghastly throat wound, blood gushing from between his fingers. Blood spattered from his mouth as he tried to scream. There was a skirmish near Stallion. Timothy snarled like an animal and then lashed out with impossible speed. His fist punched through the flesh and bone of the driver's chest like it was wet cardboard. The man's body trembled at the impalement, shock and disbelief twisting his face into a cartoonish expression.

Waving a small souvenir baseball bat, one of the car's passengers charged the deli manager but was dismissed in a heavy spray of blood. The man sank to his knees as if to pray and then pitched to the side, his face all but cleaved off in jagged gashes. His body jerked and shuddered in an obscene death dance.

Timothy snarled into the face of the man hanging on his forearm. The man tried to speak, but dark blood replaced his voice. Timothy studied him for a long moment and then stepped forward, forcing his arm further through the man. Timothy smiled, and he looked like a serpent. His mouth opened wide as if he was yawning. Cheyenne couldn't take her eyes from the man's shark-like maw. Jagged teeth filled the cavity, and his mouth stretched to impossible proportions. Timothy struck at the man's throat with impossible speed, teeth disappearing deep into the flesh. His victim's body seized and became rigid. Timothy hugged the man to him, an embrace so ghoulish Cheyenne retched. Choking on his own blood, the impaled man couldn't scream at the perverse taking of his life.

In the distance, a siren wailed faintly. The police would have no idea what kind of abomination they'd be up against.

Cheyenne glanced at Timothy, who was still chewing on the man's neck. The slurping sounds were obscene. She crawled across the pavement, skinning her palms and knees until she managed to get up. She ran blindly back into the dark alley she'd been drawn out of. Panic and fear engulfed her, so she couldn't feel her feet touch the concrete.

She dodged a set of garbage cans and glanced over her shoulder. A figure stood at the end of her alley. She knew it was him. A voice—his voice—spoke to her. Cold and emotionless, it sounded like he was right beside her, whispering to her like a lover. It teased her with the truth.

"There's nowhere to run, Cheyenne."

Part of her wanted to glance again, but a vision of him giving chase like a demonic cheetah after a young gazelle across the Serengeti only fueled her sprint.

13

When he spoke next, it was a horrible, deafening shriek. She winced at the words and the underlying inhuman hiss accompanying them. Somehow she realized Timothy's voice was not filling the air around her but dominating her thoughts from inside her mind.

"You'll beg me to drink from you over and over and over," he taunted. His tone was confident yet empty.

Her insides were squeezed in the fist of her fear. How hot pee didn't burst from her bladder and run down the insides of her legs was a Scooby Doo mystery.

She sobbed at the threat, shaking her head to dislodge the voice clinging like a bug in her mind. The violation was worse than anything she'd ever experienced. Worse than Mr. Stagg in PE class the infamous rope climbing day. No shower was scolding hot enough to rinse away the filthy reek inside her head. The alley was filled with her screams.

She didn't know when she'd run out of her low-heeled dress shoes and took no notice when she ran across the shards of a shattered beer bottle. The jagged pieces bit through her sheer black stockings and into the tender soles of her feet, but the pain couldn't pierce her terror. She hadn't thought about the Waves for a long time, but damn if she didn't wish Breeze and Bam and Nature Boy and Cartoon weren't there to kick Timothy's bony, freaky ass.

Cheyenne stole a last desperate look behind her as she neared the end of the dark passageway. Timothy's silhouette was gone. She burst blindly from the alley's other end, from shadowy darkness into a well-lit thoroughfare. The briskly moving traffic was of no concern. Terrified, she was three blind, breakneck strides into the busy avenue when the blare of car horns startled her. It took an instant to realize where she was, and a split second later she ran headlong into the side of a braking commuter bus. Her living nightmare went black.

2

A DAY AT THE BEACH

Timothy Doleman squinted behind his mirrored aviator sunglasses as he stared through the variety of traffic on the wide bike path. The teenage waitress dressed in the infamous bright yellow Pucker Up lemonade stand uniform stepped in front of him. A pause in the action of the beach volleyball game across the way allowed him to divert his attention. She blew a pink bubble the size of her own head.

"I'll have a large lemonade."

The waitress sucked the pink bubble back to her lips as she dropped her pen and ordering pad into her apron pocket. She glanced across at the women playing volleyball and then at the overcast sky. "A big lemon it is. And watch out—it's the perfect day for a sunburn for fair-skinned folk."

He smirked at her forced politeness. He was as pale as a maggot, and his black concert T-shirt didn't help his skin tone. "Good to know. I plan to stay under the umbrella." His attention returned to the volleyball match, dismissing the server.

It was hot even without the sun, with little in the way of a breeze to take the edge off. Timothy pulled the weathered envelope from his pocket and undid the clasp.

The voices of the women players carried across to him, though he couldn't always make out exactly what was being said. No matter—he wasn't spying. Not exactly.

The quartet continued to play a competitive match. Each player was athletic and attractive, drawing a small crowd of onlookers. Timothy's attention was locked onto the sun-bronzed beauty in the layered black and white tank tops and cutoff jean shorts.

Cheyenne Benjamin was all over the court, though not as fluid as normal, calling out to her playing partner, older sister, Janice. Timothy couldn't take his eyes off her. Her muscles flexed under skin glistening with sweat, and her dark, French-braided mane hung down the middle of her back to the delicious curve of her bottom. She sported a bruise where her right temple and forehead met, and her right wrist was wrapped for support.

Cheyenne stumbling across him the night before was sheer coincidence, as much as his running into Breeze's egotistical Wave brother, Stallion. The opportunity to feed on and kill a Wave was too much to pass up, though if he'd thought it through, he'd have turned Stallion and aimed him straight toward his fellow Waves. As far as Cheyenne, her fate was already sealed. She was going to be his.

After the next point, Timothy slid the contents of the envelope on the table, quickly shuffling through the stack of photographs. They featured Cheyenne, though many had been roughly doctored with scissors to remove people she shared the image with. There was a black and white of her as an infant, lying on her tummy and beaming for the camera. Their kindergarten class photo. One from his eighth birthday party. The seventh grade Halloween dance. She was dressed as an angel, and he was the devil. Both were smiling ear to ear. It was the last one where he

17

was as tall as her. There were several from high school, including one from their senior prom. He'd carefully covered her date's face with a picture of his own. It was one of his favorites despite the image of local street hero Wallace Thornton sporting the classic black tux—and not him.

He lifted the picture to his lips and kissed it tenderly, for a moment imagining the photo was Cheyenne. He leaned it against the table's umbrella pole and went back to watching the object of his affection. She made a diving save of a spike, and he nearly jumped out of his seat with excitement.

Cheyenne had sprouted another few inches during her high school years and became an all-state player. Her talent, coupled with her extraordinary leaping ability, translated well to the beach game. He'd watched her play with members of the Waves street gang years back, and she more than held her own. Now he enjoyed watching her play against her beach rivals. With the sudden upheaval of his own life, he was now in a position to more than fantasize about making Cheyenne a major part of his future. Hell, she'd be the center of his new world. The queen of his new kingdom. He could understand her reluctance to hitch her emotional wagon to the son of a deli owner. Not exactly an exciting or prestigious fantasy to set a woman's heart ablaze. Then again, short of being a rapper or a professional athlete, there was no competing against the roguish appeal of the Waves. Until now.

Street gangs among the Southern California beach communities had a secretive history. Media portrayed surfer dudes and skateboarders as the all-American end-all for young men growing up along the coast, but the beach also drew young men from all over the Southern California basin and beyond, emotional orphans looking for a new and different kind of family. Some guys surfed. Some skated. Others protected their turfs from neighboring rivals. The Bloods had the Crips. Wallace Thornton and the Waves were the Robin Hood and Merry Men of the South Bay. They'd taken on all challengers from the neighboring communities—the Shanghai Kings, the Pearls, the Mongrels, the A-Bombs, the Piranha; the list went on and on—and came out on top. Fucking Wallace Thornton. Hell, Breeze and the Waves had saved his own stupid ass the summer after high school graduation.

Timothy had known the unwritten rules and curfews, but he'd crossed into the Pearls' area of Manhattan Beach after midnight anyway. His date had wanted some Mama Italy's pizza, and he wasn't smart enough to say no. She was more cute than pretty, and he'd been mesmerized by her lacey black bra, barely covered by a sheer white blouse. He'd been at her mercy since she'd stepped out her front door.

The Pearls were an all-female gang but more than dangerous to an ordinary couple. He wasn't sure what was going to happen to his date, but he knew for a fact a dozen badass women were going to slice him to ribbons. Strangely, it had been Cheyenne who'd called out his name before a handful of Waves appeared. Breeze sauntered into the scene, enjoying an ice cream cone like a five-year-old. The leader of the Pearls was a petite beauty who sported a jagged scar that jumped over her black patched left eye, and a terrible diagonal scar across her throat. In fact, there wasn't a visible patch of pale-milk skin not covered in a myriad of healed-over slice marks. As she addressed him and his date, her voice sounded like a dentist's drill dipped in mud, but her eyes betrayed her feelings for the Wave's

19

leader. In a couple of minutes, Breeze had negotiated their release. Timothy had never felt better about buying a half dozen large specialty pizzas. And the whole time, Breeze acted like they'd done nothing more than jump started his car or something. No big deal.

Thornton was the jock with no interest in organized sports outside of boxing, and despite being plenty smart enough for college, he was just a grease monkey at heart. He had a natural charisma and seemed to make friends as easy as breathing, while Timothy hung on to the edges of mediocrity and continued to love Cheyenne from half a block away. Thornton being a nice guy somehow made it worse. Nice guys were supposed to finish last, right? Thornton somehow managed to be the world's toughest boy scout. Timothy had never heard the gang leader use a cuss word, and he was polite to a fault, especially to women. He and the gang leader should have been best buddies watching some asshole millionaire's son ride off into the sunset with her.

Sometimes he thought if he'd become a Wave he'd had a chance at Cheyenne, but he knew that wasn't true. There were some cool dudes in the gang, but only one Breeze. And it was never going to happen; his father had him working at the deli every day after school so he could learn and take over the business someday.

Wow. Owning a bakery and deli was so much better than being a train engineer or a teacher or a fireman, or a thousand other possibilities. His father had taken over the business from his grandfather and he'd take over from his father, No discussion. End of story. And the end of any dreams Timothy had growing up, no matter how many scholarships he earned.

Cheyenne dove headlong for a knuckleball serve but couldn't get her forearms under it. Sand flew everywhere, and she and her sister laughed and slapped hands as she knelt, quickly brushing sand off herself.

Tim smiled at her attempt. He loved the way she competed. She never gave in. He hoped their kids were the exact same way. Would they have kids? Could they?

The server set a large drink cup on the table, careful to avoid the pictures. Timothy tugged his baseball cap down. Even with the cloudy sky, he felt the sun's rays cooking his thick layer of sunblock.

"Will that be it for the moment?"

He dropped a bill onto her serving tray. "Keep the change."

She smiled, stepping into his line of sight. "Thanks. I'm a dime closer to that Ferrari I've been eyeing."

Timothy frowned at the woman's remark and then realized his mistake. He replaced the five dollar bill with a ten.

"Sorry about that. Wasn't paying attention."

"Uh huh." The server glanced at the volleyball game. "You could have fooled me."

Timothy reluctantly focused on the young woman for the first time. She was definitely a teenager - old enough to drive but not a co-ed. Her platinum dyed hair was boot camp short, and her skin was as tanned as any beach establishment employee. Multiple piercings adorned her ears, eyebrows, nose, and lip. Timothy was a split second from focusing back on the match when a bead of sweat raced along the server's jawline and slipped under her chin. It made its way down the center of her throat and into the ravine between her ripe breasts. Her heartbeat was strong and steady. Timothy nodded, imagining what fresh fruit she might taste like.

"Tangerine," he whispered just loud enough for her to hear. It wasn't the word as much as how he said it that made the young woman blush.

She walked away, confused about the brief interaction. Timothy's eyes drifted back to Cheyenne, but the gnawing hunger that bead of sweat caused lingered. His stomach growled and his groin stirred.

Different hungers. Same cause.

He took a sip of the pier's most popular lemonade stand. It was cold, but it tasted like ice water. He didn't care enough to call the server back. It was probably another subtle side effect of his recent ... change. Cheyenne called out the score. It was already game and match point. He'd been late getting out to the sand. Night owls needed their beauty rest.

Cheyenne jump served a dying knuckler that split her two opponents and just caught the end line tape. Cheyenne and her partner celebrated briefly and then slapped hands with the opposing pair under the net. Timothy watched her use a towel to wipe the extra sand off her arms and legs. It was time for him to go. If she caught him, there'd be drama out the ass he didn't need right now. Why screw up a good thing?

Timothy left the table and moved through the patio area to the rear of the stand. He grabbed his customized fat tire beach cruiser and headed toward downtown. Best if he made it indoors before the sun broke out. His exposed skin felt on fire. Enough fun and games.

3

YOU CANT GO HOME AGAIN

Cheyenne sat at a small window table for two at the No Doze, No Close Coffee Shop. An untouched ice water sweated in front of her as she stared across the street. Her small one-bedroom apartment sat above the Time after Time watch store.

She hadn't been home since the incident with the bus. Her sister had joined her at the emergency room. She'd only lost consciousness for a few moments, and luckily her injuries were pretty minor. She'd stayed the night at Janice's, and hung out for most of the day. She'd been able to push the events of the previous night to the side, almost as if it had simply been a nightmare. Cheyenne was able to join Janice for their regular beach volleyball date, though she hadn't been at her best. After dinner, with the sun setting during the drive home, Cheyenne became more and more anxious, and less interested in spending the night home alone. Horrible details of the night before began to plague her. When they drove past the first Pacific Grove exit sign, a cold dagger of fear plunged into her midsection. When she stepped out of her sister's car, Cheyenne was already eyeing the neighborhood coffee shop.

Unsure if Timothy knew where she lived, Cheyenne continued past the locked metal door securing the stairwell

23

that led up to the storefront's second floor. The store used most of the second floor for extra inventory, but Mr. and Mrs. Garrett, once close friends of her parents, had carved out the apartment for her. The business's high-tech security made her feel almost as safe as being Breeze's ex. At least until tonight.

When she'd walked into the twenty-four-hour coffee joint, she'd peeked up and saw the light on behind the closed curtains of her living room window. She always left a light on; she hated walking into a dark room. When the server had stopped at her table, she passed on coffee or tea and asked for a glass of ice water.

Her living room light went out before the waitress set the water down in front of her.

Cheyenne waited for the police or the security patrol to show up. Fifteen minutes passed. Half an hour. An hour. No one came to check out the intruder. She wasn't sure what to do. Exhaustion weighed on her shoulders like a heavy quilt. Another half hour passed, and her eyelids felt dipped in concrete.

Something jolted her awake. Good Lord.... She stared through the spotless plate glass, not sure what she was looking for. Her eyes searched the time store and her second-floor apartment. Nothing odd jumped out at her.

Her living room curtains parted a tiny bit. The subtle movement was impossible to miss.

She was being watched. Fuck.

She felt Timothy's gaze burrow into her, nesting at the back of her skull like a knot of hungry maggots. But it wasn't her brain she felt the larva feasting on. It was her soul.

Cheyenne wanted to run. To hide. She closed her eyes, trying to block out the infestation, but he forced her eyes open, making her look beyond her reflection and stare into the strip of darkness between her curtains. Only the desperate energy of her fear kept her from plunging into the blackness. Whatever was in that void, whatever was waiting for her, she knew there would be no return.

"*Open yourself.*" Timothy's tomb voice seeped into her mind.

The order confused her despite her instant willingness to obey. Damp, icy tendrils crept under her clothing and along her skin like a graveyard vine. One circled her throat and tightened just enough to let her know the power it possessed. A pair converged on her chest, each circling and teasing at her hardening nipples. She resettled in her chair, her thighs parting slightly. She took a sharp breath as it slithered along the edge of her panties.

"*Come to me,*" his voice directed. It was equal parts plead and demand.

A venomous stinger plunged through her skull and lodged behind her eyes. Its entrance seared white-hot, but when it came to rest, its burn turned into a numbing cold. An icicle syringe. Before she could complete the thought of who was speaking to her and where the voice was coming from, she was already rising from her seat, ignoring the necessity of leaving a tip and barely registering to take her purse. She simply did as she was told, with no hesitation or fear of the voice's absolute power.

Cheyenne pushed through the café door, and her world became a series of sensory snapshots. A car horn blared as she crossed the street, unable to feel her feet striking the pavement. The shadowy stairs to the second floor creaked under her deadened legs. Her front door swung open, beckoning like a hangman's trap door. A sliver of light—a barber's straight razor made of moonshine—sliced through the parted curtains of the living room.

She stepped into her small bedroom, her limbs heavy, her movements mechanical. Cheyenne lay on the bed, unable to do anything but stare up into the darkness where the ceiling hid. The invisible tendrils caressed her most sensitive spots like an all-knowing lover. Despite the fear pulsing through her, her body responded to the unexplainable foreplay.

The torrents of fear and pleasure inside her intertwined and then surged. Her fingers clutched at the bedspread as her hips slowly undulated. She moaned, her body betraying her, a sound that would surely be mistaken for wanton desire.

Timothy's naked form eased out of the inky darkness above her, his flesh so unnaturally pale it almost glowed. Tears spilled down the side of her face. Her fingers moved on their own, drawing the hem of her skirt up her tanned legs. Her thighs parted, offering herself. Timothy's manhood jutted from his body. His eyes glowed red like ambers of charcoal, his smile that of an insane circus clown. As his mouth opened, Cheyenne's sob was swallowed by a grunt of building pleasure. She wanted to close her eyes and look away from the impossible amount of teeth in the man's mouth, but his control of her will was complete. The first drop of his saliva seared her cheek, igniting an orgasmic explosion unlike anything she'd ever experienced. As Timothy's body covered hers, its ice-cold touch made her shudder as it seared her exposed skin.

"You are mine." The words echoed in her mind like the ringing of a demonic church bell. The creature that appeared to be her former high school classmate slithered his way down her body. Her hips rose from the bed as she

rasped for satisfaction. A pair of long, sharp fangs pierced the soft flesh of her inner thigh just above the scar from a dog bite when she was in grade school. It was hardly a kiss's distance from her moistening sex. Her eyes rolled back into her head as the pleasure erupted inside her. Her orgasm exploded with such force it caused the muscles throughout her body to seize and cramp. She cried out, as much for the violent release as her body surrendering to the violation. She knew the worst was still to come. Something worse than death. Something vomited from hell's deepest, darkest pit.

Something that felt absolutely wonderful.

God help her damnation.

———————

When Cheyenne woke, she kept her eyes closed, afraid of what she might see. The bedroom was quiet. Her mind was just as quiet, though her head ached like a New Year's hangover. The Timothy demon had vacated. When she finally gathered the nerve to open her eyes, she was alone.

She groaned as she sat at the edge of the bed. Her muscles screamed in protest. Her inner thighs were smeared with dried blood. She couldn't stop her fingers from inspecting the pulsing wounds. She remembered enough details from the night before. Her stomach clenched, a dull hunger gnawing. When she tried to stand, her legs barely supported her. She stumbled a few steps to her dresser and stared at her reflection in the broad mirror. She winced.

She looked like a used up, cut-rate party girl. But she felt worse.

Cheyenne's stomach flipped and twisted, and she stumbled into her small bathroom. She caught the front edge of her toilet as her legs gave out and her stomach ejected its contents with a splash. Her insides continued to buck and heave, but not much else came out. Her hand floated up blindly until her fingers caught the lever and flushed. She wiped her mouth with the back of her hand. She pushed herself up, the writing on the mirror over the sink catching her eye. Where the dried blood came from made her flinch.

Cheyenne took in the message. It was short and sweet and corrupted most of her reflection.

BRING HIM TO ME.

Cheyenne stared into space, thinking. Bring him …? Bring who?

The answer doubled her over at the waist. She gripped the edge of the sink, shaking her head. She would never betray the Waves, or their leader. But the throbbing twin bite marks on her inner thigh threatened consequences beyond her imagination. She felt each puncture wound oozing poison, saliva, blood … she needed to warn Breeze about Timothy and what happened with Stallion. Cheyenne would try to explain, but there was no guarantee he would listen. The news reports didn't begin to tell the whole story. And Breeze was playing house in the suburbs now.

A vampire was terrorizing Pacific Grove, and he wanted her ex-lover. And more of her. Much, much more.

4

THE ADMIRATION OF SCARS

Wallace Thornton allowed his body to relax as it decelerated on the shoreline's packed sand. The burnt orange sun blazed just above the Pacific Ocean, a breathtaking sight too often missed by exiting beachgoers too influenced by avoidance of rush-hour traffic and the lure of cheap-drink happy hours. He glanced at the Pearls' leader as she ended their sprint. Her tight striped shorts were at least a size too small, even for her petite frame, so the bottom edges of her well-rounded ass peeked out to the world. Her dark hair was a combination of razor-close punk and a thick crew wave whose bangs fell across her eyes. Her streak of independence was a mile wide.

Cecilia "Moon" Aubrey turned, hands on hips, smiling. "You've been off the sand too long. Almost had you."

Her raspy growl of a voice didn't match her appearance. It was the most major of the long-term effects of her accidental fall during high school. The Wave leader dropped to the sand.

"Uh huh. I felt your breath on the back of my neck."

Moon smacked him on the shoulder as she walked past. "It's just a matter of time before I run you down. Especially since you've gone totally straight."

He couldn't stop from turning and watching her walk away as he rubbed at his right knee.

She spoke without turning around. "So sad when you can't get what you want. I hear it causes man cancer."

Wallace "Breeze" Thornton rose to his feet and brushed the sand off. "I admire Picasso but don't necessarily want one on my wall. You need a healthier guy anyway."

"Someone healthier than you?" She placed a hand on his lean, muscular chest.

It still rose and fell from the exertion. The current leader of the Waves made his sweat-soaked white T-shirt look like a tux.

Moon let her eyes drift up and down his six-foot-two frame. "I'm not into pedigree pony boys." Her nails scraped down his torso, lifting away at the elastic waistband of his running shorts. She didn't miss his six-pack rippling away from her teasing touch.

"Be careful, this is a family beach."

"More people have fucked on this beach than at the drive-in."

"But not before sunset," he corrected.

Her eyes twinkled. "We're practically outlaws. The rules of civilized man don't apply to us. Doesn't matter. You have no interest in this piece … of art."

Breeze grunted and wiped a hand over his sweaty, clean-shaven face.

Moon pouted. "Well, I'd say you're no fun, but I know better." She stood on her tippy-toes and teasingly bit at his lower lip. "Better watch out. Opportunities don't come around every day." She started up to the beach. "Not like men and buses."

"Cute." Breeze felt the effect of Moon's nip throughout his body. She was as beautiful as her name, scars or no scars. "Hey, you ever see Joseph Poole around?"

Moon stopped walking but didn't turn around. "Why?"

"No reason. Just wondered."

"Not lately. He works in Long Beach at one of his family's jewelry stores. We were never close after the accident. You know."

Breeze stared at her until she seemed compelled to continue.

"He only came to the hospital a couple of times. He never called. And once I returned to school and the Frankenstein stuff started, he wouldn't even look at me in the halls. I think he was ashamed and felt guilty for what happened."

Moon turned and looked out over the ocean. For a moment Breeze felt invisible.

"He took my virginity at his house that night before I fell three stories from his attic bedroom window into his mother's glass greenhouse. The fact that he'd lied to my face about his parents accepting me—you know, the poor girl from the wrong side of the tracks with the father doing time and the mother who died from an overdose. I bet you didn't know they initially called the police because they thought they'd come home in the middle of a break-in. Crazy, right?"

Eventually her gaze fell back on Breeze. His eyes dropped from her face and took in the scars not covered by her outfit. They seemed infinite, like her own private collection of skin stars, varying in length from tiny to sizable. Somehow, after all the years, they seemed to fit

31

her, like alien tattoos created just for her. Scars and eye patch or no, Moon was a unique beauty.

"Penny for your thoughts?" she asked quietly.

"I think they fit you." Breeze moved close enough that anyone watching would have known they were more than friends. Or once were.

"I could do without them, but they certainly add to my tiny but lethal intimidation factor."

"Now who would be afraid of a little thang like you?"

Moon stepped close enough to slow dance. "Only 'bout ninety percent of the population."

"I love these monthly work road trips."

"And the wife is okay with them?"

"I have her blessing. No secrets in our marriage. She knows the water is in my blood." Breeze used a fingertip to gently trace across one of Moon's larger shoulder scars.

"Plenty of scar freaks out there."

"Sure are. But I'm a lot more than that."

Breeze kissed her on the top of her head like a little sister. "Yes, you are."

Moon noticed but let it pass. She also noticed Breeze stiffen. She turned away from the ocean's edge. In the distance where the walking and biking paths paralleled the shore, a smattering of beachgoers and tourists milled about. Her eyes settled on a single, out of place image, causing her emotions to veer in a different direction.

A huge, dark-skinned Black man stood next to Breeze's minivan. Moon smiled at the sight of Leonard "Bam" Matthews. causing her a split second of hesitation as Breeze loped across the loose sand.

Bam pushed his round-framed glasses up his broad nose as the two gang leaders moved toward him. His gray business suit barely contained his bodybuilder's physique.

It was probably a safe bet Breeze's six-foot eight, three-hundred-pound friend was the largest head librarian in the world.

Breeze pulled up a few steps from Bam. A sheen of sweat covered the big man's smooth skull.

"What's going on?" The de facto leader of the Waves asked.

"Bad news, man," Bam whispered, his baritone syrupy smooth. "Real bad news. Moon."

"Sun Block." Normally the big man would have smiled at the pet name, but his expression, half-hidden behind sunglasses, remained stoic. The shit must be bad.

Breeze glanced at Moon, but she offered no hints.

"Stallion's dead. Murdered last night." The big man stepped closer. "Cheyenne was a witness. She's holed up at her place. She sounded really scared. I think we'd better check on her."

Breeze let out a deep breath, glancing back at the setting sun. He shook his head. "Can you call Crater? I've got a long drive to the valley. I've already pressed my luck with the beach run."

"No problem." Bam nodded. "Good to see you despite the suck-ass news. Give the wife a kiss for me."

"Hit the road," Moon said, squeezing Breeze's arm. "That traffic ain't getting any better." The Wave nodded. He really needed to head home, and Moon was right. The rush hour traffic was going to suck.

The threesome moved toward the parking lot and their respective vehicles.

5

HOW LEGENDS ARE BORN, HEROES UNMADE

The northbound traffic was so miserable Breeze would have thought it was pouring rain. Multiple vehicles were pulled over to the far right with their warning lights flashing, hoods up, or getting assistance from law enforcement. Breeze crept along in his minivan, rarely reaching thirty miles per hour.

Unable to find good music on the radio, his mind startled to drift. With the baby due soon, he knew his involvement with the Waves was coming to an end. His white-hat street gang had dominated the last several years of his life. They'd become his second family. So many wonderful, exciting and flat-out funny times. Being the guardian angels of Pacific Grove had gotten them a segment on *60 Minutes*. Law enforcement, while not completely on board with their existence, grew to tolerate their positive effect against street crime in their beach community. What started out as an exercise in simple street survival against neighboring communities gangs became a valued position.

Breeze's mind shuffled through memories like a deck of playing cards. The fights. The girls. The adventures.

Getting elected the Waves' first and only leader. The list went on and on.

So many great memories, but his thoughts kept reaching back to the night he foolishly challenged the powerful Piranha gang to the infamous one against three, winner-take-all battle royal.

The rivalry between the Waves and the Piranhas heated up as the Waves rep ascended, forcing their way into recognition. The leadership of the Piranha began to squawk, eventually insulting and then threatening the female members of Breeze's family. The Wave leader was seething when the gangs showed up for combat at a park near the border of their communities.

Breeze's anger boiled over as soon as he saw the red and black attired group on the playground equipment. Each gang was at full strength, limited to thirteen members, and absolutely no weapons were allowed. Straight hand-to-hand combat. The old-school shit Breeze was raised to love.

Without thinking it through, he broke away from his Wave brothers and stalked straight toward his rivals. Their leader, Lobo, and their gang's enforcer, Rico, met him by the huge children's sandbox.

Before he'd thought the challenge through, Breeze had shouted at the Piranha that he'd take on their three best fighters, the winner winning the rule of their bordering territories. The challenge drew some laughter, and their leader, the leather-tough Lobo, immediately accepted.

Breeze would never forget the look on their faces when he informed the group. No one spoke for a moment, and then Bam whispered, "What?" His expression was comical. Breeze had never seen it before or since.

The truth was, if it was going to be a regular three-on-three challenge, Breeze wouldn't have even fought. Logically, the participants would have Ant, Bam, and Jester. It wasn't that Breeze wasn't a good streetfighter or wasn't tough, but it wasn't much of a secret that he wasn't the strongest, smartest, or toughest Wave. He acknowledged that fact. But he also knew why he was their leader, and that night something inside him screamed for him to step up.

Even as the Waves were letting his challenge sink in, some of their attention drifted toward the playground equipment. Breeze remembered Crater saying the word shit, and then Breeze looked over toward the Piranha. They'd chosen their three, with no surprises. Their leader, Lobo, was an automatic choice. Breeze had seen him fight a couple of times. He was street hard, and not too different from Breeze and his garbage-can fighting style.

Their second choice was their enforcer, Rico. He was covered in ink, including a set of flames that crawled up his throat, crossed his cheek, and ended on the top of his clean-shaven skull. He was average height but bull strong. He was a pure heavy hitter with jaw-breaking power in both hands. If Rico landed one square, it was good night. He didn't go in for much wrestling or martial arts stuff. The third killer fish was almost as big as Bam, and one of those dudes that, despite being in his late teens, looked like a grown-ass man. His gang name was Monstruo, and it fit him to a tee. Sure, his sheer size was intimidating, but it was his hands that held one's attention. They were oversized even for a dude his stature. Breeze remembered watching them slowly flex into fists from across the distance. Breeze had only seen him fight once, and the thing that'd struck him was he was quick on his feet, not slow and lumbering.

36

He was a brute with some wrestling skill. He wanted to get his hands on you.

"Wish me luck," he'd said to his brotherhood and then strode out to meet his first opponent.

Breeze guessed it'd be Monstruo, and it was. It was going to be impossible to do much damage to their big man while staying out of range. Breeze thought about the things the Piranha had said about his family, especially his sisters, and he grimaced as he covered the ground between them.

Monstruo smiled as the Wave leader approached, his fingers finally bunching into enormous fists. A step or two from the brute's range, Breeze had a flashback from the beginning of the movie *Troy*, when Achilles had taken on the giant warrior from the opposing army in a one-on-one match. Fists up in a basic boxing defense, Breeze stepped directly in front of Monstruo and then ducked to his left, anticipating the big man's move. Monstruo threw a looping right hand that flew over Breeze's shoulder. Momentarily off-balance and defenseless, Breeze stepped in and hammered a straight right of his own at the juncture of the giant's right jawbone and ear. Monstruo roared at the blow, stumbling as he fought to keep his balance. Breeze, taught to fight by his ex-Golden Gloves champion father, stepped right after him, throwing a nasty left-right combination that spilled Monstruo onto a picnic table. Breeze stayed on him, darting forward and throwing a knee into the man's sternum. Monstruo struggled to get back to his feet as Breeze bounced away. The cheers from both gangs filled his ears, surrounding him like an action movie soundtrack.

Monstruo snarled, angered and embarrassed, and then rushed the Wave leader, arms wide like a grizzly's. Breeze dropped and swept him at the knees, the big man tumbling and sprawling in the loose dirt. Breeze dived on top of him, grabbing him by the hair and slamming his face into the ground multiple times. Monstruo tossed Breeze off his back and staggered to his feet, his face covered in dust, blood streaming from his shattered nose.

"Come on!" he roared, lumbering forward, spitting blood.

Breeze smiled at him and then at Lobo. He moved straight toward Monstruo, darting to the right just as the big man took a vicious swing. It missed, but Breeze didn't. He stepped in and rained a barrage of punches to the face and midsection of Monstruo, chopping away at the man like a sharp axe on a large oak.

Monstruo fought back, landing a couple of glancing blows, but he seemed to know defeat was closing in. Breeze boxed the man until all he could do was try to defend the much quicker Wave leader. Driven back toward the other Piranha, a series of blows dropped him to a shaky knee, and Breeze finished him with a hammering right-left-right combination that dropped him at his leader's feet. Monstruo rolled weakly from side to side, encouraged to get up from his gang brothers, but he couldn't do it.

Breeze had pointed at Lobo and then raised a single finger into the air. "That's one," he'd called out to the cheers of his Wave brothers.

"Five minutes," Lobo had called to Breeze's back, his accent thick with simmering anger.

"I'm counting the fucking seconds," Breeze had yelled back, smiling at his fellow Waves.

Breeze knew he'd gotten a little lucky. He'd figured very few people had stood up to Monstruo, and fought him straight up. The next two fights would be completely different and tough as hell.

Breeze leaned back against a tree and tried his best to relax. Too many voices were in his ear about Rico, the Piranha enforcer, figuring Lobo would be the anchor fighter for the challenge. Breeze watched the mauler getting loose. He'd been the one running his mouth the most about Breeze's family. It was going to be a pleasure making him swallow blood and teeth.

"Ready?" A Piranha called across the way.

Breeze got to his feet and started toward the opposing gang. Several strides across the clearing, Breeze was surprised to see Lobo, not Rico, stepping forward. He'd taken off his gang shirt, displaying a large lightning bolt down the middle of his chest ending below the waistline of his black jeans.

"You're good," he said as he approached, slowly raising his hands chest high. One hand curled into a loose fist while the other extended, still open.

Breeze nodded. "You and your man made this personal, so you both gotta bleed."

"Then make me bleed, *puta madre*," Lobo answered, and it was on.

Lobo was like a piece of metal, and he'd had a lifetime of street fighting experience to fall back on. Breeze took nothing for granted and quickly got a taste of the Piranha's skill.

Lobo stepped in and threw a double-up left jab to grab Breeze's attention and then dropped down and hammered a punch to Breeze's midsection. He then sliced an elbow into the Wave leader's face. It caught Breeze across the eye, sending him backward in a defensive retreat. Lobo moved with him, jabbing and then dropping into hooks and upcuts. A punch slammed into his ribs and then an uppercut cracked against his chin, sending Breeze sprawling to the ground. Breeze heard the Piranha roar with approval while his own Waves were coaching and encouraging him back to his feet. Breeze took another pair of punches as he tried to get back to his feet and then rolled away, his brain calculating, sizing up his opponent.

Lobo stood back cautiously, not foolish enough to rush into a mistake. Breeze took a deep breath and then shifted his stance to southpaw. He circled into Lobo's right hand, which seemed to throw off his timing. Lobo mirrored his change of approach, easily avoiding Breeze's range-finding jabs. But before Lobo could set his own attack, Breeze threw another jab and then dived into a wrestling takedown.

It took Lobo by surprise. When his back hit the dirt, he squirmed and fought to get back to his feet while Breeze took advantage of the man's lack of grappling skills. In seconds, Breeze had Lobo's right arm extended and locked. Lobo hissed and cursed, his brain registering the sudden danger he was in, knowing he had no answer to his predicament. Breeze snarled something to him through clenched teeth, but Lobo didn't understand until he felt the jolt of pain jump from his wrist through his arm up into his shoulder.

"Tap or I break it!" Breeze shouted.

Lobo's eyes widened and he squirmed like a mouse on a glue trap. He couldn't surrender in front of the others.

Breeze didn't hesitate. He snapped Lobo's wrist like a graham cracker and then twisted and pulled his shoulder out of socket. Lobo howled with electrifying pain as Breeze released him and bounced to his feet a safe distance from the Piranha leader. His gang was mostly quiet, shocked by the sudden turn of events. To his credit, Lobo pushed his way to his feet with a painful cry, his right arm hanging useless. He shook his head, trying to clear his eyes of the searing pain blurring his vision.

He raised his left arm and made a fist. "Come on, motherfucka! Come on!" Lobo challenged, inching forward.

Breeze dropped his hands and looked past his opponent to Rico. "It's over."

Rico shook his head. "He's not out, and we don't hear him surrendering."

Breeze looked at Lobo. "Give up or I'll break your other arm."

When Lobo didn't answer, Breeze started forward. Just steps away, Lobo's fist opened and he extended an open hand.

"It's ... it's over."

Breeze stopped and Lobo nodded to the Wave leader before turning and rejoining his gang.

Breeze looked Rico straight in the eye. "Five minutes, piss ant."

Rico started forward, but his brothers held him back, getting in his ear, trying to settle him.

Breeze turned and rejoined his Waves, his ribs barking on both sides.

The five minutes felt like thirty seconds. Ant tried to give him some basic combat advice, but it was hard to focus over the searing ache that came with each breath. When he heard 'ready' called out from the other gang, Breeze had to admit he wasn't anxious for the final match, but Bam caught his arm and reminded him about Rico's bullshit. His ribs didn't stop hurting, but his focus locked back in.

The Wave leader had always thought it was funny that the leader of the Piranha didn't fight the anchor match, instead leaving it up to the gang's enforcer. Breeze had certainly been roughed up in the second encounter but still had gas in the tank.

Rico was no piece of Kleenex, and he went after Breeze hard and fast. Breeze took a punch that opened a nasty gash over his right eyebrow, and there was no good way to keep the blood from affecting his vision. The constant swiping at the wound kept him cautious early on. His fists were sore and achy. His aching head hadn't taken away from his focus, instead making it razor-sharp. Breeze didn't take the fight to Rico, instead fighting defensively, wrestling more than punching. Rico was a straight-ahead brawler, but not a deadhead. He wanted no part of a wrestling match. Breeze saw the taunting leer on Rico's face, and he still heard the ugliness the man had spewed about the women in his family. Breeze took a couple of steps back and raised out of his takedown crouch. He reverted back to his boxing stance.

"Come and get your ass beat," Breeze said, waving the man forward. Rico's bully ego rose to the surface. Breeze flinched at a flare of pain from his black and blue ribs, and that was all the invitation Rico needed.

Rico almost connected on a wild haymaker to Breeze's head, but he'd anticipated the tactic, ducking under the grazing blow and driving an uppercut just below Rico's sternum. The punch lifted the enforcer just off his feet, the air whooshing out of his lungs. Breeze slipped his left hand around the back of the fighter's head and steered it down into his knee. Rico flopped onto his back, his nose gushing blood. Breeze followed him to the ground, mounting him and driving straight punches into the man's face. Left, right, left right, left, right. He grabbed the groggy man's head by the hair and threw a vicious scissoring elbow, breaking his jaw. Rico struggled weakly to protect himself, but it was no use.

Once Rico was at his mercy, Breeze waved everyone back. He stood over the semiconscious Piranha and literally kicked his face in. Rico was defenseless, but Breeze was hellbent on making a point. Rico was carried away by a pair of his gang brothers, his mouth a jagged, bloody mess.

The Waves had been yelling and jumping around like they'd won the Super Bowl, not as careful as Breeze would have liked them to be with his battered midsection. After that night, the Waves became the number-one gang, and Breeze's life was never the same.

The smile on his face lingered as he filed away the wonderful memory, but it quickly faded when he realized he still wasn't half way home. Shit.

The gate to Cheyenne's upstairs apartment was unlocked. That immediately struck a nerve. Crater led the way, bouncing up the stairway in a series of effortless leaps. He waited for Bam to lumber to the top.

"Stallion is really dead?" Crater was still digesting the news Bam had reported. The librarian nodded. Silence hung in the air like cigar smoke.

"Stallion gets offed. Terrible but within the realm of reason," Bam said.

"But the rest … of this shit about Cheyenne being involved … and attacked …"

"Not involved … she said she was … working. Saw the whole thing from across the street."

Crater and Bam paused a few steps from Cheyenne's apartment. The door was open. An unpleasant chill climbed Crater's spine.

"Fuck." Bam said. He suddenly wished he was out of his business clothes and wearing something easier to fight in. He slipped out of his suit jacket as Crater reached out and softly rapped his knuckles against the wooden door.

"Cheyenne?" He spoke quietly. The silence was far from inviting.

Crater stepped into the apartment's gloom. No lights were on. With the sun almost down, the place would soon be pitch dark.

"Cheyenne?" he called out again. Halfway across the living room, a cloying smell reached his nostrils. Like rotting fruit.

"Crater?" Cheyenne's voice was like a dying bird. It came from his left, the darkness of the bathroom.

Bam tossed his dress coat onto the couch and balled up his fists, ready for anything to leap from the shadows.

As Crater eased toward the bathroom, that smell grew more putrid. His brain tried to identify it. Not bad diaper or hot, dried piss like from under one of the beach's piers. Not sour milk either. Nor was it an animal carcass on scalding pavement. Rotting fruit was closer, but not exactly right. As he reached inside the darkness for the light switch, the assault on his nostrils was savage. He winced, covering his nose and mouth.

The light over the mirror and pedestal sink flicked and then blazed on. Crater wasn't sure what to expect from the sight of his leader's ex-girlfriend, but the image caused him to fall back a step.

Cheyenne was pressed back against the wall between the sink and the toilet, her bare legs pulled against her

44

chest. Her hair looked like a crow's nest after a hard winter. When she raised her head to look at him, her eyes were sunken and glazed, her complexion pale and drawn. She appeared to have not slept for a week as opposed to a single night. She looked to be only wearing a T-shirt, and vomit was crusted down its front. The first thought that flashed through his mind was *strung-out addict*.

"Cheyenne?' Crater said, coming out much more of a startled question then he'd meant.

She groaned and hugged herself tight. She mumbled something he couldn't understand as she stared at her bare feet. Then her arms floated up to him, pleading.

Frozen, Crater stared at his former high school classmate as Bam, ignoring the stench and her rough condition, slipped past him and gently scooped her into his massive arms.

"Are you hurt?" the big man asked.

She shook her head. "No ... yes ..." She pressed her face into his meaty shoulder. "I don't know exactly."

Bam turned to carry her out, but she shook her head again. "No, don't. Just put me in the tub. I need a bath."

Bam glanced at Crater and then whispered in her ear. "Are you sure that's a good idea? If you were ... attacked, you know ... evidence?"

"I wasn't raped," Cheyenne said. "At least not exactly."

"Not exactly?" Crater said. "What the fuck happened?"

Bam lowered her into the tub like a child.

"Let me get cleaned up and I'll tell you everything," Cheyenne said, laying her hand against Bam's cheek. He kissed it gently. She looked over at Crater. He'd suffered horrible acne through high school, so his adult face was forever pitted and scarred. His appearance never seemed to bother women much. Half his head was shaved clean, while the other half was dark and wavy to his shoulder. "Just … please don't leave me alone."

"We'll be right outside the door," Bam whispered.

"Don't close the door," she pleaded, a stark fear bleeding into her voice.

"Okay. I'll stand right outside." He opened the bathroom window to vent the awful stench.

"Thank you." She sobbed.

Her hand trembled slightly as she reached out to turn on the water. Her back to them, she stripped off the fouled T-shirt.

The two Waves stepped out of the room. They couldn't help but look at each other, concerned at their discovery. Almost as an afterthought, Crater walked over and turned on the living room light.

Cheyenne didn't say a word during her bath. Minutes stretched out in the uncomfortable quiet. Eventually the two men heard movement from the tub and then water draining, and then the subtle rustling of her robe from behind the bathroom door.

"Need help?" Bam called out.

There was a pregnant pause, and then she cleared her throat and squeezed past the men into the living room. She was still pale, but she looked better with her hair hidden in a towel while she was wrapped up in her bathrobe. She certainly smelled better. She dropped to the couch, one sweatpants-covered leg under her. She looked out the living room window into the early evening. Her expression subtly sank.

She looked at two of the men she trusted most in the world. "I'll tell you everything, but I don't think you're going to believe me."

"Sure we will," Bam reassured her.

Crater wasn't so sure.

Cheyenne took a deep breath and then started. Her attention never left the living room window.

Minutes later, when she'd finished, Crater rose to his feet and wandered around the room.

"I'm not crazy, and I'm not lying!" she cried, flinging open her robe and jerking at her sweats' knotted drawstring. She pushed the sweats down her legs, and a second later a familiar sickly sweet smell wrinkled the men's noses.

"What the fuck is that?" Crater spoke.

And then they both saw it. Rivulets of dark blood and pus oozed along Cheyenne's inner thigh. She turned and kicked the wounded leg up so her heel rested on the edge of her couch.

The twin bite marks, fiery red and puckered, were a couple of inches apart. The area around the bite was swollen the size of a large egg. Black veins spiderwebbed from its center.

"What in dear God...?" Bam folded to a single knee, staring in disbelief.

The swollen, pulsing wound throbbed to match Cheyenne's heartbeat.

Mesmerized, Bam leaned forward, his hand drifting toward the ugly wound. His fingertips floated just over it. "Does it hurt?" he asked, nose wrinkling at the odor.

"Yes ... and no. It doesn't hurt to touch it, but the ... the ... discharge, it burns. And you smell it. You smell the poison leaking out. He fucking bit me!"

"The dude from the deli," Crater said. "Thomas ... Theodore ..."

Bam was drawing a complete blank.

"Timothy. Timothy Doleman," Crater recalled. He glanced at Bam. "We saved his skin from Moon and her girls a few years back. Breeze brokered the legendary pizza deal."

The big man nodded. "I remember the pizzas but don't really remember the guy."

Crater couldn't take his eyes off the crazy wound.

"He doesn't really stick out in a crowd. Nice enough guy, but pretty average. Barely won the war with acne. Wasn't a jock or a brain. Had a serious thing for Cheyenne."

"What? When?" Cheyenne said, pulling up her sweatpants.

"He was digging on you when I moved here."

"We were just school friends."

Crater met her eyes. "Trust me, he wanted more. But you and Breeze got together."

"Uh, the class reunion stuff is great, but let's get back to Stallion's death and what this guy did to Cheyenne," Bam said.

"Hey—I admit the bite is ugly as hell, but a vampire? Really? Come on now!" Crater stalked about the room.

"What else do you want me to call someone who, who hypnotizes me, forces me to come to my apartment, and then doesn't rape me but bites me, and ... and ..."

"And you watched him handle Stallion with one hand?" Bam questioned.

"Yes. It was crazy. What Timothy did was unbelievable, but I saw it."

"He punched through a man's chest?" Bam asked.

"Yes, I did."

48

The statement came from outside the living room window. Had the window been cracked open all this time? Cheyenne clutched her knees to her chest and started whimpering the Lord's Prayer.

"Good evening, gentlemen. Just like old times."

Crater and Bam stared at the window. Neither moved a muscle. Their chests didn't rise with a drawn breath.

"You probably don't remember me, but I know you. At least one of you."

A moment later, an arm reached down from above the window, and long, spider-like fingers clutched the open window's bottom. The knuckles were boney knobs, and the nails were longer than they should have been. The hand hardly looked human.

The window was pulled upward until it was wide open.

"Bam—you got your nickname as the high school's All-American left tackle. You used your football scholarship at UCLA to earn a master's degree in library science. You're now running the downtown Los Angeles public library, one of the largest on the West Coast.

"And you, I don't know. I was expecting Breeze, the legendary leader of our local street gang. Officially, the Waves no longer exist, but unofficially, with the assistance of the Pearls, a few Waves like yourself still keep the local streets safe."

"And you're Timothy, the deli owner's son," Crater replied, taking a step toward the window. "Still have a hard-on for Cheyenne?"

"Bright boy, but you seriously need to see a dermatologist. I bet our Cheyenne had to tell you who I was. But no matter."

Something was outside, and Crater and Bam's imaginations began to run wild. Any number of terrifying monsters were set to leap through the window and attack them. It sounded like nails dragging across the building's brick exterior. Was something crawling toward the opening?

"I can taste your fear, you know. Each has its own particular flavor, like different types of apples, or ice creams."

The living room and bathroom lights went out, plunging the apartment into darkness. Cheyenne cried out as Bam jumped to his feet.

Timothy chuckled. "I can't blame you for being afraid. I'm not the scrawny little man I was a few days ago. I've evolved into something more. Much more. Cheyenne thinks I'm a vampire, and that might be the closest term to describe what I'm becoming. I can understand your trouble believing her fantastic, though truthful, story. I did kill Stallion and those other insects last night. I did start the process of making Cheyenne my forever queen."

Crater took another step toward the window. "Forever queen? What the fuck are you talking about, Timothy?"

"I don't like the way you say my name. It sounds like you're spitting out phlegm. I know your mind is full of questions, many of which would be answered if you'd simply look out the window, but you won't. Neither will Bam. You feel cowardly for your hesitation, but I actually applaud your survival instinct. So many of your old rivals would have rushed the window only to find their deaths, while you will live to fight at least one more night, depending on the dwindling limits of my mercy."

Crater glanced across the dark room at his friend but couldn't make out his expression. For the first time in a long time, Crater didn't know what to do.

Timothy continued. "All right. Enough of this chit chat. I came to feed. Cheyenne?"

"Please ... please don't make me," she pleaded.

Even in the shadowy gloom, both men could make out her struggle to remain on the couch. She was losing. Cheyenne couldn't stop her limbs from unfolding against her will. She stood up, wavering on her feet.

"I'm going to feed on her right in front of both of you, so you'll have no doubt what you're up against when our gangs finally meet."

"Please ... stop him." Cheyenne begged, willing with all her might not to take one wooden-legged step after another.

Before either man took action, Timothy's voice floated into the room. "If you attempt to stop her, you'll force me to come inside and slowly slaughter you all. Not like your friend Stallion, who I killed with the exertion of flipping a light switch."

Halfway across the room, Cheyenne reached out, her fingers clawing at the air. "Help me."

Bam took a couple of quick steps and grabbed her hand.

Soft applause came from outside. "So brave. But stupid. Call your dog off, or you'll watch me devour each and every one of his steaming organs."

"We can't let him ... do this," Bam said. "We're not cowards."

Unable to look his friend in the eye, Crater stared at the open window. "We don't know what we're dealing with, man." He shook his head. "Let her go."

51

The monster outside laughed. "Wise decision. The weight of leadership can be quite the burden, especially to those who aren't up to the task."

Releasing her hand, Bam yelled in agony. The window allowed for just enough light for him to see Cheyenne's shattered expression as she was drawn closer to her doom.

"Feeling powerless, Bam? Guilty? Weak? Useless?"

Cheyenne stepped up to the window. Her desperate sobbing filled the room. Like a rusty robot, she bent into a shaky squat and reached out.

"I'm sorry," Crater whispered.

And then she was gone.

Neither man had time to move before Cheyenne was back, screaming.

She was hanging outside the window, upside down, her head and upper torso in clear view. She was thrashing about like a fish caught on a hook, her arms flailing, her scream filling the night air. She stared, wild-eyed, into her apartment at the two men. Suddenly her scream cut off and her body sagged limp, but she continued to stare inside, her expression slack and empty.

A foul sucking sound was just loud enough for them to hear. Bam sank to his knees while Crater covered his ears, but they couldn't escape the assault on their souls.

Cheyenne began to pant, and then she giggled like a mischievous child with a terrible secret. She stared into the dark apartment, straight into Crater's eyes.

"I'm his whore and I'm going to cum." Her panting grew faster and louder, and then her body shuddered and shook. Her fingernails dug into the flesh of her palms, drawing blood during the powerful climax

"Nooooooo!" Crater cried out as he lunged for her, but Bam grabbed him in a bear hug he couldn't escape.

Cheyenne giggled as she recovered, and then the process started again.

Bam released Crater, who folded to his hands and knees, struggling to block out the nightmare when Cheyenne was dropped in a heap back inside the window.

"Enjoy her company while you can. She's not made for unlimited refills. Good night, gentlemen."

Bam scrambled to the window, plunging his head outside. Crater crawled to Cheyenne's side. She was barely conscious.

Bam pulled himself back inside. "Nothing out there, man! Fuck!"

Crater scooped up Cheyenne and headed to her bedroom. "Call everyone. We've got to get ready."

Bam crossed the room and grabbed his phone from his jacket pocket. "I'm calling Papa Midnight too." His voice shook with anger and guilt. He realized he was alone in the room. Then the gut-gnawing fear returned, and he wasn't alone anymore.

Crater called out from Cheyenne's bedroom. "And call Breeze. Figure out a way to get him back down here 'cause we need him."

The phone felt heavy and hot in his hand. Bam would have smiled if the circumstances had been different.

Crater was right. They needed Breeze, but getting him to return during the current circumstances wasn't going to be easy.

6

THE NEW KING OF THE STREETS

Timothy staggered away from the roof's edge, a toothy smile dominating his face. Chest heaving, laughter finally exploded from his lungs as he danced around, pure happiness fueling his movements. He'd done it. He'd intimidated the great Bam. No—he hadn't intimidated them. He'd frightened them, like children gathered around a campfire being told a ghost story. He'd scared them. He felt their fear pulsing off them with each heartbeat.

The kings of Pacific Grove's streets were no more. No one was going to stop him and the Master from taking over the South Bay beach communities, establishing a foothold, and eventually conquering all of Los Angeles. Then Southern California, the West Coast—they'd spread and dominate like a super virus.

And Cheyenne would be his whore-queen for eternity.

He'd never been a very good dancer. Not that he'd had many opportunities. No one really danced at homecoming or prom, and he wasn't a nightclub guy. But right now he couldn't stop his body from dancing to a mixture of internal music, and it was amazing how good he felt. With no one watching, he could just be free. Tidbits of dance movie scenes flashed through his head, and he was suddenly the star of each of them. He was the shit now—not Breeze. And he did it on his own, without a gang, though that would be the next step in the Master's plan.

Timothy snapped his fingers to the beat in his head. *Footloose, Save the Last Dance, Flashdance, Dirty Dancing.* He and Cheyenne were next up to stroll down the *Soul Train* dance line …

He froze, mid-dance move. The Master was suddenly in his head.

"Timothy." The Master's voice was monotone and soulless. "You celebrate an insignificant triumph. You might as well still be human."

Timothy's head dropped in shame. All his glee evaporated. "Please forgive me. The past is hard to let go."

"Enough of your emotional entanglements. Go build my army."

"Yes, Master."

And just that quickly the Master was out of his mind. Timothy winced at the sudden departure but was glad for the exit. He looked up into the new night sky and gauged the time. He had a busy night ahead. He sprinted to the rear of the roof and leapt off into the darkness above the alley that ran four stories below. He knew he couldn't fly, but when he dropped to the pavement and strolled away, he certainly didn't complain about what he could do.

PEARLS BEFORE SWINE

Several cars and scooters filled the well-lit parking lot of the former Zippy Cola distribution building on the main drag of Fin Reef, one of Pacific Grove's neighboring towns. Bam's black pickup pulled into the lot just ahead of Crater's classic Triumph motorcycle. The large, blacked-out windows greeted the Waves as they approached the first closed service bay door. Bam carried Cheyenne's limp body like a basket of straw in his massive arms. Before Crater could press the service bell, the metal door started up.

The rising door didn't take long to expose a small crowd of women. It was an eclectic and diverse group. The women were multiracial and represented every height, build, and hair color. Their postures appeared relaxed, but Crater recognized looks could be very deceiving. The Pearls might have been an all-female gang, but they were not to be underestimated. Moon was as tough as she was beautiful, and her right hand was downright dangerous. Cheyenne would be safe here.

"We need your help," Crater said, stepping inside before he was invited.

Bam followed. The Pearls neither opened their ranks nor blocked their path.

Crazy Mabel appeared from an adjoining room. "What's going on here? You Crater?"

"Where's Moon? We need to talk to her right away."

Six foot tall and big boned, the Latina, Crazy Mabel, stepped to the front and peered at the semiconscious woman. "Somebody shut the fucking bay door. Shit. Hey—ain't this Breeze's ex?"

"Yeah, she was attacked. We didn't think it'd be safe to take her to my place or the hangout."

Crazy Mabel looked at the Waves. "She looks strung out. This ain't no women's shelter."

Bam took a couple of steps forward but the closest Pearls closed ranks.

Crazy Mabel looked Crater in the eye. "We know Breeze and Moon are buddy-buddy, but she ain't here."

"When do you expect her?" he asked.

Crazy Mabel smirked. "I'm not her fucking secretary. She's out. And you ain't leaving that sick bitch here. Uh-uh."

"Crater." Bam growled softly. "We don't have time for this shit."

"Hey—we didn't call you. Get the fuck out you don't like our company."

Crater yanked out his cell phone and made a call. "Moon? Yeah, it's me. Bam and I are here at Zippy Cola, and Mabel is being a harder ass than usual."

A few seconds passed, and then Crater held out the phone to the big woman. "Moon wants to talk to you."

Crazy Mabel mumbled a few cuss words and then snatched the phone out of Crater's hand. She gave the Wave a soul-withering glare before spinning away.

"Moon? Uh huh. I hear you." Crazy Mabel tossed the phone back to him. "She said be nice. She's on her way."

"Is there someplace we can lay her down?" Bam asked, straining to be polite.

Crazy Mabel frowned. "Take her to the bunk room. Make her comfortable."

The big man started forward, but a handful of Pearls took her from his arms.

Crater and Bam eyeballed Crazy Mabel and the remaining couple of Pearls. Crazy Mabel looked the two men up and down. Especially Bam. Her smile was sincere, but it didn't look like she'd had a lot of practice doing it.

"That library hasn't kept you out of the gym." When the big man didn't respond, she continued. "What do you bench? I just forced up 225 this morning."

Bam snorted at the statement. "Two twenty-five? At your height? Impressive."

"Gotta be strong enough to handle what comes my way. Being an enforcer ain't eating ice cream."

"Amen to that, little sister. God might be busy, so—" Bam started.

"You gotta be able to count on yourself," Crazy Mabel finished.

"Damn. You stalking me?"

Crazy Mabel laughed, and her face softened. "You all's high school yearbook is lying around here somewhere. It was your senior quote. Wished I'd used it for mine."

Suddenly the service bay door started up, the loud rattle filling the momentary silence. The Pearl gang leader climbed out of the shiny sports coup. Her outfit was simple but stunning, each piece eye-catching. She moved in the four-inch black pumps like they were tennis shoes. Her black jeans looked like shadows perfectly wrapped around the curves of her legs and ass. Her top was black lace with a deep scoop at the neck, reaching well short of the low-rise black jeans. She didn't believe in using much makeup, but she also didn't need it. Her red lipstick shouted kiss me if you dare.

As she entered the light of the loading bay, she wore her multitude of scars like body paint. She waved over her shoulder, and the Audi rolled back as the bay door descended.

"What's going on?" But before Crater could speak, she wagged a finger in the air. "Just a guy from the straight world dipping his toe into the deep end of the pool."

Crater nodded. "We have drive-in movie shit to share. We brought Cheyenne—"

"What! You brought Breeze's ex-bitch here? To my place?" Moon closed the distance between them. "You must be crazy or fucking desperate."

"Desperate beyond your worst nightmare," Bam said.

Moon looked at the two Waves, picking up the serious vibe. "All right. Mabel, you hang tight. You others head back inside. I can't wait to hear this bullshit, fresh from the prison shower end."

Crater watched the Pearl members disperse, and then he opened up. "We're talking vampires," he started, not sure how else to begin their fantastic tale.

Moon glanced at Mabel, who shrugged. "What the fuck are you talking about, vampires? Some new gang making noise?"

Crater shook his head like something was loose between his ears. "No. No. We think we're dealing with something like the real deal."

"You know, creature of the night, fangs," Bam added, trying to paint a clearer picture.

Both women stood quiet for a few seconds and then burst out laughing.

"Hey," Crater said, but the Pearls just kept laughing. Frustration got the better of him and he darted forward, stepping well into Moon's personal space. "This isn't a joke."

Crater hadn't been the only one to move. Crazy Mabel had drawn a .38 and had it pointed at his face. Moon glared at the Wave, the tip of her gleaming switchblade less than an inch from Crater's crotch.

Bam slowly raised his hands to his shoulders. "Everybody chill," the Black man whispered. "We didn't come here to make the evening news."

"Back the fuck up," Moon hissed, "or we're all going to the ER."

Crater stepped back. Mabel kept her gun on him. Hesitantly, Moon put away her blade.

"All right then. Let's start again, but with the truth this time. Mabel?" The Pearl enforcer eased the gun down, securing it in the waist of her jeans.

"We're telling you the truth, Moon. Cheyenne has been attacked a couple of times by someone ... or something acting like a fucking vampire. No joke."

Moon looked at the two men, and their expressions made her not want to laugh anymore.

"You can look at the bite marks yourself."

Moon glanced at Mabel and nodded. The big girl led the way to the bunk room.

Cheyenne was still out of it when they entered, and Bam circled around to reach her bedside first. His bulk sagged the mattress, and he eased the covers down her pale, perspiring frame.

"Damn," Crazy Mabel burst out, grabbing her nose.

Bam gently eased her thighs apart, and Moon was startled at the wound.

Bam spoke. "And before you try to rationalize it, that ugly bite is not from a rattlesnake or a brown recluse."

"Fuck a spider—it would have to be the size of a dog to have fangs that far apart," Mabel observed.

"We watched her get fed on less than an hour ago."

Moon looked at Crater. "You just watched?"

Crater rubbed his hands through his hair. Shame kept him from meeting Moon's accusing gaze. "It's all crazy, I know. And we think we know who did this, if what Cheyenne told us is true."

Crazy Mabel backed up a step. And then another, unable to take her eyes off the pulsing wound. "What else could cause that, Moon? Jesus, Mary, and Joseph."

"She needs a safe place to hide. She was attacked both times in her apartment, but we don't think she'd be safe anyplace attached to us. The hope is he won't track her here." Bam pulled the covers up and tucked them in around her.

Moon frowned at Crater, but Crazy Mabel beat her to the punch. "You *hope* whatever bit her doesn't track her here? Fuck you!"

"A minute ago you were laughing your ass off," Bam said.

"A minute ago I hadn't seriously thought you looked like you were afraid the fucking boogeyman was under your bed."

"Can she stay here or not?" Crater asked Moon.

She pursed her lips and blew out a deep sigh. "We'll watch her tonight, but she's out of here by tomorrow's sunset. That's it. I'll make sure a couple of Pearls watch over her until you pick her up."

"Thank you." Bam struggled to smile.

61

"And let's not be slow sharing information when you get some. Knowledge is power," Moon instructed.

The Waves nodded and followed the Pearls back through the soda plant.

"Nice setup," Crater commented, taking in the unique clubhouse.

"The Queen Mary wasn't available," Moon said, leading the way.

"Sorry to interrupt your date," Crater said.

"No worries. He wasn't wearing my favorite cologne."

"You look great, by the way," Crater said.

"Wow, you're really observant." Moon pressed a button, and the bay door started up with a loud metallic rattle. "Good night, gentlemen."

Crater and Bam stepped into the parking lot. The door lowered again.

"Sweet dreams," Moon teased with a wink, blowing them a kiss. The bay door slammed shut.

"Don't even start," Crater warned as they headed toward their vehicles.

"Who, me?" Bam shrugged. "I was actually wondering if Crazy Mabel was lying about her bench press."

"Really? That's what you were thinking?"

Bam started to climb into his truck but stopped. "You ever seen Mabel cleaned up?"

Crater stared at the Wave second-in-command and then shook his head. He sat on his bike.

"Hey, I'm just saying, she might clean up real nice."

"Sure—a grizzly in heels. A regular circus act."

"And people mistake you for a nice guy. Wow."

"I prefer dates I'm not afraid to stick my hand through the cage bars at. You're the risk taker. At her size, her lump of coal might become quite the diamond."

Crater pulled on his helmet & started the bike.

"And she's got like three sisters, right?" Bam said, but Crater was too busy zooming out into the busy boulevard traffic.

Bam jumped behind the wheel, gunned his pickup and followed.

8

YOUNG AND OLD ALIKE

The next morning Timothy Doleman stood outside the oversized wooden doors of The Enchanted Castle Preschool. Looking every bit the medieval building despite its lesser scale, Timothy found the two story daycare and its occupants especially invaluable to the Master's plan.

Tangerine, the punky server from the beach lemonade stand, stood next to him. She stared, trance-like, at the side of his face.

Behind his dark sunglasses, he stared up into the security camera and smiled.

A young woman's voice greeted him from the callbox. "Good morning. Can we help you?"

"Hi. My family has recently moved into the area, and we'll be in need of daycare services. I was hoping we could get a tour of your facility."

"Do you have an appointment?"

"I'm sorry. We do not. Normally, my wife would handle something like this, but she won't be joining me until next week."

"Just a moment, please."

After a pause the security door buzzed, allowing the pair to enter. The interior continued the exterior's motif.

Though brightly lit, the hallway lighting was decorated like torches.

An attractive, post-college-aged woman of Asian descent stepped around the receptionist desk. She wore khakis and a black promotional T-shirt. Her smile had a youthful sincerity, but its charm was wasted on him. He smelled the blood flowing through her like homemade spaghetti sauce simmering on a stove.

"I apologize, but our director is currently engaged, so we can't offer you a tour today. I can give you some literature that should answer your basic questions, and I can schedule a tour before the end of the week. How does that sound?"

As she stepped close enough to offer the pamphlets, the mild ache in Timothy's crotch matched the pulse of blood flowing through her carotid artery.

The vampire took off his sunglasses and gazed into her eyes. The young woman's arm hung out in the air waiting for him to take the offered paperwork. Her body shuddered as if a chill was passing through her, but her eyes never left his, even as an inky darkness turned his eyes black.

"I need you to secure this building so no one can enter or exit. I also need you to disable the automatic police and fire alarms. If anyone comes to the front door, explain there's an issue with the security system, which has affected the front doors. All incoming calls via the switchboard are to be ignored and allowed to go to voicemail. If a problem presents itself, merely think about it and I will know. Understood?"

The receptionist wavered slightly on her feet. She nodded once, tossed her hair, and then offered her throat. Timothy bit her, though not deeply to feed, but only enough to inject his select venom. The young woman hissed in disappointment as he withdrew his mouth and fangs.

Tangerine licked her lips and moaned with hunger.

"But first, show us to the oldest children."

She smiled and started down the main corridor, dropping the already forgotten daycare's literature on the floor. The wound on her neck continued to drain, though the punctures were already sealing up.

"The four- and five-year-olds have two classrooms," she said.

"Lovely," Timothy said, his alligator smile returning as his lengthy tongue licked her blood and saliva off his lips. He glanced at Tangerine.

"You can have a room of your own. Remember—sedate for control. We'll have plenty of time to feed and turn."

This was going to be so much fun. He felt the Master's approval.

———

Bam's truck pulled into the fast-food parking lot. He had successfully wrangled his adopted grandfather, Papa Midnight, into coming.

Bam climbed out from behind the wheel and quickly moved around to the passenger side to assist his guest. No one could decipher the age of the ninety-something based on his wardrobe. The senior wore a nice sports coat and jeans, with a crisp white dress shirt. His old-school Converse high tops perfectly completed the ensemble.

Papa Midnight dropped to the ground without a stumble, and the diminutive man turned to face the warm sun. His complexion was even darker than Bam's, and the wrinkles dominating his face were the only clear sign of his age. His dark eyes twinkled behind his small round glasses. A white-haired goatee surrounded his warm smile. "That sun feels so good."

Bam could not stop his smile. "Always good to see you, Papa. And I think the sun shines at Sunset Dunes too."

The old man laughed, sincere and infectious. "You're always surprised to see me this side of the dirt. And you know those early risers always take up the best benches."

"The devil don't want you, gray beard, and God's afraid you're going to take heaven over."

"Could be, could be," the senior mulled over as Bam's massive arm swallowed him up.

After fetching a bag of breakfast food and drinks, Bam sat with the man at an outdoor table. The warm sun did feel good.

"Thank you for coming out, Papa," Bam said with a smile as he passed out the food. He set a large coffee in front of his senior guest.

"What? And miss this banquet of breakfast debauchery? Not on your life, young Leonard."

"Well, I touched on the subject of our discussion last night and you didn't laugh."

Papa Midnight took a bite of his bacon, egg, and cheese biscuit. He moaned in ecstasy. "So, so good, yet so, so bad for you," he said around chews and a sip of coffee.

Bam enjoyed the old man's satisfaction. The two ate until Papa Midnight spoke up. "So, you think there's a vampire in Pacific Grove?"

Taken a bit off guard, Bam stopped eating mid-bite. Papa Midnight's directness shouldn't have been a surprise. The former director of the Los Angeles Police Department

Informational Services Division pulled at the brim of his FBI ball cap.

"We're not sure, really," Bam said, anxious about sounding crazy.

"Well, you must think so, at least enough to ask the smartest man in the world about it."

Bam chuckled and went back to eating. "It doesn't sound totally whack to you?"

"Shit—the lack of three-cylinder cars when gasoline is four dollars a gallon seems crazy to me. Vampires …" He paused to enjoy a bite of crunchy hash brown. "This ain't their first rodeo in the Southland. At least I don't believe so."

Bam's eyebrows arched in disbelief. "You're kidding, right?"

"Look, I'm not talking about black caped, turn into big bats, but … blood drinking, blood worshiping crazies, sure."

Bam continued to chew and swallow, relieved and intrigued.

Papa swiped his mouth with a napkin. "There are hundreds of reports involving aspects of vampirism. Never been a shortage of whackos with blood fetishes. Charismatic cannibals, Elizabeth Bathory followers, blood cults, Dracula wannabes who become psychotic and violent …"

Bam broke in. "Wait—Elizabeth Bathory?"

"The Blood Countess. Fifteenth, sixteenth century Hungarian woman accused of torturing and killing hundreds of young women. Rumors say she bathed in her victims' blood as a perverse fountain of youth. Crazy bitch."

Bam nodded. "They've made movies from her legend. She was a serious freak, but she didn't have supernatural powers, right?"

"Just the power of position and money. Nothing from beyond the grave."

"Yeah, but the cat we're dealing with has power. Powers that seem vampire-like. Strength, hypnotism, and he fed on Cheyenne right in front of us."

Now it was Papa Midnight's turn to stop mid-bite. "What'd you say? This freak fed on your friend right in front of you?" The old man's gaze glared with condemnation. He dropped his food back on its wrapper. "You couldn't stop him, or you didn't stop him?"

Bam's eyes dropped to the table. He ran his hand over his clean-shaven skull. The men sat in silence, slowly returning to their breakfast.

"Damn," the old man spat under his breath, too stunned to accuse the young man of cowardice. He knew him too well. Or at least he thought he did. His worried expression finally drew an explanation.

"It was just crazy." Bam struggled to find the words to make his mentor understand. "I let Cheyenne down." He shook his head.

He reached across the table and looked into Papa Midnight's eyes. "I haven't been that scared since the shadow man in my closet made me pee the bed."

Papa Midnight took a sip of coffee and then returned to eating. "Well, whatever nutcracker crawled out of Hell and ended up in Pacific Grove, maybe you ought to leave it to the police. This might be beyond the Waves."

"If we're right, the cops won't understand what hit them until it's too late. Plus, this man—thing—whatever—

has made it personal. It knows us, Papa. We're part of whatever this thing is doing."

"I can get you all the information you want, but this sounds like something personal between you and this lunatic. You just said something very important. If he knows you, you know him. He's using his knowledge of you to get the upper hand. Fight fire with fire. If you can figure out the end game, it'll make it easier to fight him. I wasn't there, but kid, you have to know you're dealing with a human monster, not a real vampire. It's just some whack job with a few tricks up his sleeve. You'll see."

"Makes perfect sense coming from you."

Papa Midnight took another drink from his coffee. "You gonna eat that last hash brown?"

Bam glanced down at his remaining breakfast item. He passed it over to his family friend. "It's all yours, old man," he offered with a smile.

"Don't mind if I do." Papa Midnight grinned. He gobbled the crispy potato patty up and then washed it down with the last of his coffee.

"Now that's a breakfast. Beats the heck out of oatmeal and banana slices."

Bam frowned at the thought. "Note to self—die young."

The table was silent for a moment, and then both men burst out in laughter.

Papa Midnight chuckled "You keep messin' around and you'll get your wish, son. But seriously, I need you to listen. Let me do some research, but in the meantime, keep a few possible facts in mind. Generally speaking, he's gonna be strong. Real strong. Hyped up on drugs, whatever. And fast. Quick like a cat. Likely being a sociopath, he'll be merciless like a spider or a shark or a scorpion. He might be able to hypnotize or control minds, but usually out of charm and suggestion and by using drugs on his victims. If he's totally sold into his vampire fantasy then he'll probably be weaker during the day but don't count on the sun killing him because he's not a supernatural creature. Wouldn't get stuck on using a wooden stake to kill it—you ought to be able to kill him like any ordinary man, and you won't need to take any extra steps to make sure he stays dead. Remember, he just believes he's a vampire, and a large part of his power is getting others to believe it too."

Papa Midnight looked up, squinting at the fiery white sun. "Damn that sun feels so good. No wonder old dogs like to lie in the sun. I might have to start getting up before noon more often."

His gaze fell back on the young man, who hung on every word. "And they may or may not believe they survive by feeding on human blood. Most quote/unquote vampires are mentally ill freaks with a blood fetish."

"Most?' Bam questioned.

Papa shrugged. "The world is full of weird people. Weird creatures. Weird ass circumstances. Not everything on this earth is meant to be explained. I've never seen a real vampire and I would bet your guy isn't a soulless, undead creature of the night either."

The Wave nodded, letting the man's words sink in. "So what you're saying is, expect some crazy shit, and believe what you see."

Midnight glanced at Bam. "Who says you're just another pretty face?"

"Just the people who know me." Bam chuckled.

Any lingering negativity dissipated like early morning beach fog. Bam gathered up the trash while Papa excused himself to the restroom. When he returned, the duo

71

headed to Bam's pickup. Bam's phone buzzed and he gave it a glance. "I'm headed to the shop to meet the guys."

Papa Midnight paused before climbing back into the truck. "You did call Breeze, didn't you?" The old man waved away Bam's assistance and disappeared inside the cab. Bam nodded. "Yeah. I reached out. Left him a voicemail. Not sure he'll show. He was just down here, and he has a family now."

"He'll hear the importance in your tone. He'll show. You'll need his leadership."

Bam climbed in behind the wheel and started the truck. It was time to get ready to play, and no one played harder than his leader.

9

ROLL CALL

An assortment of vehicles occupied the All Night
Garage parking lot. Breeze recognized some
and guessed at others. He steered his newer minivan into
his unofficial parking spot by the entrance, hardly able
to contain his excitement. He pushed through the front
doors, the shoulders of his sports jacket nearly filling the
threshold. He was not surprised to find the doors unlocked.
All members of the Waves knew the security code, which
was randomly changed by the security company.

With the sun shining through the oversized stained-
glass windows, it was impossible to tell if the brightly lit
room was powered more from natural or artificial light.

What used to be the main office of his grandfather's
automotive repair garage was filled with a dozen or so early
twenty-somethings. The chatter ceased and all eyes turned
on him.

He smiled, scanning the room. They all wore
their black and aqua leather Wave member vests. His
belongings were still packed from the move to the valley,
and he suddenly felt out of costume. He was the only one
not wearing or carrying their colors. He shook his head,
looking down at his own sports jacket, white dress shirt,

crisp khakis, and shiny brown dress shoes. He rubbed at his clean-shaven jaw and chin.

Breeze greeted everyone. "Gentlemen."

"Cool Breeze."

The smooth, syrupy voice belonged to the long and lean Lone Star transplant with the dark sunglasses and ornate cane. Breeze made a fist and bumped it against the knuckles of his blind friend.

"Good to see you," the Texan joked, smiling from ear to ear.

"Nice to see you, Longstreet," Breeze fired back, grinning as the other Waves moved in to surround their leader.

The welcoming energy swept over Breeze, relaxing him, reminding him he was home. His eyes darted among the other young men in the office. He checked through his mental roll call.

A young Tarzan look alike dressed in an Armani suit had his Wave vest in his hand. He slapped Breeze on the shoulder. It was Surgeon, a Palisades rich boy banished by divorce to the South Bay.

"Goodwill?" Breeze asked.

"Laguna Beach. Best selection."

Whisper, a skateboard junkie who loved Wham! music, shook Breeze's hand. The man's chest stretched every fiber of his George Michael tour T-shirt. His oversized custom board hung from his other hand. He pushed back the scraggly mop of jet-black hair with frosted white tips. "Chief," he said with the greatest respect.

Sailor was next. He lived on his grandfather's boat in the neighboring marina. He'd set up his own fishing and tour gig.

Gypsy, a military brat who finally found a home, saluted Breeze from across the room. Breeze nodded with a grin and saluted back.

Trojan, a Southern California University football fanatic, was covered from head to toe in SC gear. He appeared to have not missed an upper body day at the gym in quite some time. Trojan sported a thick handlebar moustache.

Jester, Samoan born with absolutely no sense of humor, nodded solemnly. It was as happy as Breeze had ever seen him. He was thicker through his chest and torso than any man Breeze had ever met. He'd been shot several times, but no one had been lucky enough to seriously wound him. The baby boy of thirteen children, Jester's family might actually be the toughest gang in South Bay. Eight sisters and all.

Jim/Joe, an identical twin who took his dead brother's name, hugged Breeze tight.

"Nice to see you man. Joe says hey," Jim/Joe said.

"Hey right back," Breeze replied sincerely, ruffling his friend's hair.

The night of their initiation into the Waves, Joe was hit in a crosswalk by a drunk driver. He didn't survive the ambulance ride to the nearest ER. Jim said his brother's spirit had appeared at the foot of his bed before dawn the night he'd died and had hardly left his side since. Of course, everyone thought he was crazy with grief, but he was too good a friend not to support. Then again, Papa Midnight always acknowledged Joe when Jim was around.

Bogart, whose given name was Humphrey, smiled and waved from the office's back wall. He wasn't big into crowded spaces. Girls loved his eye patch, which they usually thought was fake, but he'd lost his left eye in a nasty surfing accident. The patch he wore today was black with a yellow smiley face.

Ant, the five-foot-tall mixed martial arts fighter, jumped on Breeze's old work desk. "Didn't want you to miss me." The Jamaican smiled, his braids tight against his skull. Pound for pound he was the biggest badass of the Waves.

He dropped to the floor and then nearly tackled the Wave leader from overexuberance. The two jostled like big and little brothers, laughing like school kids.

Crater, the group's resident poet and parkour master, lightly bumped his forehead into Breeze's. "Good to see you, Wally."

When Breeze's life took him away from regular participation with the gang, Crater stepped into the breach. Crater was a good guy, solid and thoughtful, but wasn't who Breeze would have guessed to step up. Breeze knew Bam couldn't fill the void because his job in downtown LA wasn't flexible enough to allow for all the late-night street running.

"You still driving the Mustang?"

"Oh yeah," Breeze replied. "I keep it parked right next to the minivan." Laughter detonated in the room. Ant howled and crumpled to the floor. Breeze just stood there, a sheepish grin on his face. He scuffed his shoe over a shadow he mistook for a janitor's miss.

"Damn. You must be in love," Surgeon said, shaking his head.

Jim/Joe spoke up. "Dude, you should have been at the wedding. Breeze's wife is even prettier than—"

The room got quiet, like someone flipped a switch. "Dumb ass" was muttered under someone's breath. It was a subject best left alone.

Jim/Joe, caught in no-man's land, stared at the floor. "Well, fuck you. She was."

Uncomfortable silence filled the room. Movement came from the back of the room.

Zero, the ponytailed Japanese bike messenger, was the last to greet Breeze. Even when Zero smiled, there was always an undertone of sadness, anger, or contemplation. "Breeze."

As usual, the Wave leader couldn't read the man's tiny smirk.

"Zero." Breeze instantly recognized how serious he sounded compared to the others. It was also an odd time to remember he'd never known Zero's real name.

"Glad you could make it," Breeze offered, warmer.

The bike messenger nodded. "When the big man reaches out, it's serious shit."

When Zero used the words "big man," Bam leapt to mind, but everyone knew Breeze was always going to be the gang's big man until the day he died.

"Not seeing any grease under those fingernails," Zero said.

Breeze gave a double take. "Yeah, not under the hoods as much. Mostly paperwork now. Admin stuff."

"Our boy is making his way in the grown-men club," Surgeon said. "There's nothing he can't do. He's the magic man." The group agreed.

Breeze pursed his lips and took a deep breath. Everyone settled in, finding a place to sit or lean.

Others, like Stallion, had lost their lives too early. Gaucho died in a nightclub fire in Tijuana. Cartoon was killed during the Las Vegas mass shooting carrying a young girl to safety.

Slice had moved to Florida for college but wound up becoming a drug mule. He was shot and killed by DEA agents. The Bauer twins, Black and Blue, both drowned during a white-water rafting accident.

Breeze's gaze drifted around the room, touching the eyes of every Wave before settling on the floor at his feet. He slipped back into his leadership role as easily as he'd pulled on underwear this morning.

"I spoke with Bam and Crater, and they filled me in on the situation. They both did an excellent job acquiring intel and, well, staying alive to tell the tale."

Breeze took his time and told his gang everything. When he finished, the room was dead silent for a long time.

Ant looked around the room, taking in odd details of the office while avoiding his fellow Waves. "Are you fucking with us? I mean, like we're on some sort of prank show or something?"

"This is no prank," Zero said.

"Breeze didn't leave his pregnant wife to play games, gentlemen," Crater said, rising to his feet.

"This is crazy, boys." Jim/Joe shook his head. "But we all believe Breeze and Bam and Crater, bat shit or not. I'm in up to my eyebrows." The lone twin stood quiet for a few seconds, slowly nodding. "Joe says vampires are real as heart attacks."

The room dipped into another brief quiet. The Waves could hear a vehicle pull into the parking lot.

Bam pushed through the front doors soon after. He filled out his Wave vest like it was painted on. No matter what size he chose, it always appeared to be a half size too small. He hadn't lost an ounce of his intimidation factor.

It wasn't hard to read the room. The big man hugged his best friend tight. "You told 'em?"

Breeze nodded.

Bam smiled. "If it's any consolation, Papa Midnight believes it and is going to help with some research."

The room broke out in a mixture of murmurs.

Breeze quieted the room. "Hey—we're not gung-ho teenagers protecting our turf anymore. We're not talking about a trip to Prompt Care for some stitches. We're talking life or death. Doleman killed Stallion without breaking a sweat, and I think he was sending a message, and we've received it loud and clear. We're a group, not a military unit. I'm not laying out orders on this one. This is strictly a volunteer effort. Everyone is free to walk, with no hard feelings. But everyone needs to understand, this ain't no street fight. We're talking about killing … people, things. I don't know what to call them—"

"Vampires," Zero said.

"That's so fucking crazy. Really guys?" Bogart said, shaking his head.

"No crazier than the rest of this screwed-up world. Mother Nature runs a weird lab," Bam said. "Let's not forget, humans are barely different from chimpanzees genetically. Why not another offshoot of humans?"

No one raised a counterargument. Bam's subtle nod to Breeze was apologetic.

Breeze took a deep breath. "And I'm talking about a volunteer effort because I can't be a part of this right now."

The stirring and murmurs around the room ceased.

"Judi is close to her due date, and I can't take any time off because of my upcoming paternity leave."

Longstreet piped up. "And getting killed before your baby gets born would be sort of a bummer." It was just enough of a joke to break the tension.

Breeze chuckled. "It would be shitty."

"Do you know the sex yet?" Jim/Joe asked.

"Nope. We want to be surprised. I painted the nursery in neutral colors—green, yellow, and gray."

"You should have called; we would've helped," Jim/Joe added.

"I could have used it too. But I think it's kind of a husband/dad thing I needed to do. I know you all got my back."

Jester, the thick-chested Samoan, shook his head. "Breeze—the man who took out the top three Piranha to keep us all out of the ER—is painting baby rooms and taking paternity leave. Now that's what's crazy."

For a split second, Breeze almost thought he saw a grin play at the corners of the mouth of the humorless Jester. He blinked and it was gone.

"We can handle this batshit without you," Crater said, attempting to ease the pressure off their leader. "You've always been there for us. We'll take care of this while you take care of your new family."

"At least until the DNA comes back," Longstreet said. The room burst out in laughter.

"Hey," Breeze jabbed back. "My wife loves taking care of strays, but she's not blind." The laughter jumped to another level.

"When that baby arrives wearing Ray Bans, we'll see!"

"Deal," Breeze finished.

He looked around the room. "The leadership for this mission will continue as currently structured, with Crater filling in the top spot and Bam remaining the vice and the enforcer. They'll keep me in da loop, but it's their show to run."

A pair of hands floated up. Surgeon and Gypsy. Breeze nodded to the senior of the two.

"No disrespect to Crater," Surgeon started.

"None taken," Crater said.

"But if things are seriously starting to look like you and Bam are going straight full time, I think we ought to move toward an election so we can settle into a more stable hierarchy."

Agreeable noise sounded around the room.

Breeze nodded. "That's a fair and reasonable direction to take. As much as I love you guys, my life is more and more up in the valley. I know Bam loves splitting his time between LA and here, but there is something to be said for leadership based here at home."

He glanced at Bam, who smiled in agreement. "Let's get through this vampire thing, and then we'll gather again and hold an election. Everyone should be eligible for any spot."

"Including you," Ant said.

Breeze's smile was wistful. "I've loved being a Wave, but I think my time is coming to an end." He glanced at Crater, who nodded subtly. "It's probably long overdue for Crater or someone else to lead without the shadow of prior leadership hanging over them. Plenty of guts and brains in this room. We'll make the right decision and move forward."

Gypsy spoke up. "If you leave, what happens to this place? Will we need to find another hang-out?"

Breeze immediately quashed any rumors. "I own this property outright. It'll always be our home long after we've all stepped away and a new generation of Waves have surfed the Pacific Grove shoreline. Believe that."

Claps and whistles and cheers filled the office. Jim/Joe shouted, "Breeze for president!" and the room burst into hoots and loud laughter and mirth once again.

Breeze smiled at the mock nomination, making eye contact with Bam and Crater. His Wave brothers had no idea how much he wanted to stand with them against whatever this crazy threat was to their community. It almost sounded like fun in a crazy way. It had been a while since he'd skinned up his knuckles, but he had a real life now.

Family first. Even before the second family he'd help create several years back.

10

THE LAST SUNSET DU N

After Bam dropped Papa Midnight back at the Sunset Dunes, one of the top luxury senior living communities in the South Bay, he was lucky enough to claim a nice sunny spot on a bench close to the community's entrance.

A steady stream of walkers returned from their morning strolls, along with a steady flow of family members coming to visit loved ones. A natural night owl, Papa was rarely out of his room prior to high noon and regularly just made it to the dining room prior to its one o'clock seating deadline. Who knew the mornings were so busy?

But on the opposite side of the early risers were the nighthawks like himself, and Sunset Dunes turned into a whole different world after the ten o'clock news.

Papa Midnight found himself drifting in and out of a light doze, the sun's warmth acting like a gentle lullaby to his mind and achy joints. His late breakfast allowed him to skip lunch, and he spent hours on the bench watching the world go by or watching the dark insides of his eyelids. Both were satisfying.

As the afternoon drifted toward dinnertime, his bowels and bladder demanded his attention. He couldn't remember the last time he'd gone a whole afternoon

.ng to take a piss once or twice. Reluctantly, he
...is feet, relinquishing his spot. He wasn't halfway to
.. front entrance when he glanced back and saw a blue-
haired beauty had parked her behind in his spot. No going
back now. Relief was more important than wooing.

The usual early diners were already gathering. He navigated through the hallway traffic, walking against the majority flow. He made it to the elevators and rode up to the third floor where his apartment awaited. His was the end unit, so his balcony faced the busy boulevard the multiple building community sat on. The weekend nights were usually entertaining, and on the warm nights he'd sit outside and watch the world move past. Sometimes it was a late-night road racer putting miles on his bicycle, or a group of fun-loving motor scooters, or a street racing *Fast and the Furious* wannabes exploiting the straight six-lane avenue. The speed limit was thirty-five, but only the mother and fathers jogging with their baby strollers went that slow.

After a successful trip to the bathroom, he took a seat on his balcony. Before he knew it the gentle caress of the cool sea breeze put him to sleep.

When he startled awake, he was disoriented for a moment, but sure enough, he'd slept through sundown and into the star-filled evening sky. He checked his pocket watch, but it was too dark to read. When he went inside the clock on his kitchen wall read 8:20.

Shit. He'd missed his dinner reservation.

Strangely, he wasn't as hungry as he'd have guessed. Breakfast with Bam had been half a day ago. He didn't bother to check the fridge; between his meal plan, delivery menus, and every decent spot within a three miles radius, meals were never a problem. Choosing what to order was always tough, but pizza popped into his mind first, and his stomach growled at the thought of a deep-dish pepperoni from Sharkey's Pies. Now, if he could just find his glasses ...

Minutes later, when he'd discovered them propped on top of his head, he put in his order. Something nagged at him, a vague strangeness he couldn't quite put his finger on. As the night went on he'd figure it out.

He did realize he hadn't checked his answering machine all day, so he did. No messages.

Maybe he ought to change the greeting again. It always seemed like after he changed his greeting, people called and left him messages, like his recording was fresh bait or something. He always liked a greeting that mentioned mortuaries. It was macabre, but he found it amusing. Most women didn't, but they'd leave messages anyway. His buddies thought it was a hoot. Well, the buddies above ground that still had their wits about them. Too many of his friends were either dead or so mentally absent he couldn't have a two-minute conversation with the poor devils. More than one sat in their wheelchairs all day, wearing adult diapers and bibs. So sad. Papa Midnight prayed every night to not end up that way.

He glanced up at the array of framed photos on the wall. Most were black and white. He grinned at the old boxing photos. Long before he became Papa Midnight, he was Wendell "Razor" Leaf, a top-rated welterweight boxer on the East Coast. Memory still as sharp as a tack, glimpses of his past flashed through his mind. He knocked out eight of his first ten opponents. He won a televised match on *The Wide World of Sports*. He once spared against Sugar Ray Leonard when he was entertaining a comeback. A fluke ice skating accident cut his budding career short.

85

Broken wrist and forearm and a badly dislocated elbow. That was it. Over just like that.

Then again, the accident happened on the second date with his wife, Charlene. She'd driven him to the ER and stayed with him until she had to leave for work. She'd been one of the first female subway train conductors in New York City. She'd cried when he told his boxing days were over. Not because her potential cash cow was dead, but he knew she understood how much he'd loved it. After rehab, she'd talked him into going back to school, and this average high school student blossomed into a honor-roll college graduate. He went on to get his master's in computer science, and the rest was history. He landed the LAPD gig, and she padded her retirement with a cushy consulting job with Metrolink.

And then liver cancer stole the love of his life way too early. They'd never made it to Paris ...

He sighed deeply. She'd been gone for years, but the pain still sliced his soul.

He looked at the clock. He wasn't a big TV watcher, but his boozy neighbor, Dolores Finch, was a big *Murder, She Wrote* fan. Her little dog—what was that mongrel's name?—yapped through the show every night like clockwork. The show should have been on, but not a peep from next door. Maybe they'd gone out. Seemed odd, but no skin off his nose. Wasn't gonna complain about a quiet evening.

Papa Midnight headed to his bedroom to change into some sweats and slippers. He didn't know why he bothered to watch the news. It was the same old stopped-up toilet of dirty politics, natural disasters, and the passing of COVID-19 crap. His thumb twitched to turn the boob tube off, but an ugly local story caught his attention. A young female reporter with the looks of a Los Angeles Rams cheerleader stared into the camera, and her sincere expression of alarm matched the tone of her voice. Uniformed officers swarmed around her like moths to a porchlight.

"Detectives at the crime scene have no information yet on this bizarre and potentially dangerous situation here at the Enchanted Castle Preschool in Pacific Grove. Back to you, John, in the studio."

The camera lingered on the reporter for a long second, and Papa Midnight was sure the young lady was going to cry. What was the deal happening at that preschool? He switched channels and another attractive reporter was stationed outside the preschool, whose building was very much a castle. He'd been by it many times but for some reason forgot what business resided inside. This reporter could have been a Bond girl back in the day.

"Law enforcement is investigating a potentially dangerous situation here at the Enchanted Castle Preschool. Parents arrived at the school late this afternoon to pick up their children, only to discover a deserted building. Officers from a variety of law enforcement agencies are investigating. A canine officer is on the scene. There's been no official statement, so the preschool has not been designated as a crime scene. Reporting live, this is Taylor Forbath, Channel 6 News."

Papa Midnight frowned. He glanced at the wall clock and frowned more deeply. It'd been almost an hour since he'd ordered his pizza. It normally got delivered within forty-five minutes by a college kid named Pill. The senior usually gave the kid a twenty dollar bill for the $14 pizza.

He snapped off the TV in frustration. The surrounding quiet blared like a fire alarm. He quickly called the pizza place but the line was busy. He grabbed his wallet and decided to head down to the main entrance to meet the delivery guy.

Papa Midnight stepped out in the hallway and thought he heard the soft click of a door closing. "Hello?" he asked, glancing at the neighboring doors.

Nothing. No blaring televisions or loud phone conversations. He started down the hallway toward the elevators, and the soft giggle of a small child leaked out from an apartment down the wing. He paused, listening. He hadn't seen any children, but someone had company. Good for them. Grandchildren were a blessing.

Charlene and he had never been blessed with children of their own. They never went to see a doctor. As the years passed they just continued to love each other and live their lives.

The elevator opened and he stepped on, reaching out to press the button for the first floor. When he stepped out, no one was waiting to get on. The hallway was as quiet as it was upstairs. Unlike his upper floor, the ground-floor lighting had already been dimmed for nighttime. As he wandered toward the main entrance, the silence followed him like a shadow. He didn't pass anyone, nor was anyone outside.

No one was having conversations, or taking a walk before turning in, or heading back to their apartment after an evening out.

The main entrance atrium was deserted. The usual classical background music had been turned off. A resident was normally at the concierge desk chatting away, but no one was there. In fact, he couldn't hear the voice of the front desk employee. Out through the automatic double doors, the parking lot was dark. No cars were parking, pulling up, or driving away.

No. A car was parked across from the entrance.

Papa Midnight glanced at the concierge desk. The high back chair was empty. A subtle, quiet noise came from the administration offices beyond the front desk. The sound barely registered in his ears. He stopped walking and the sound stopped. He looked out the front entrance and concentrated on the vehicle with the flashing emergency lights. Something odd was mounted on the roof.

A big fin. Sharkey's Pizza.

Where was his delivery guy? If the desk sent him up, they would have passed each other.

The odd, soft noise started again.

"Hello?" No answer.

The noise stopped, and then the nighttime lighting flickered and went out.

Papa Midnight's breath caught in his chest. Before the thought of hurrying out the front doors to the major street beyond, the parking lot lights dimmed and died. A black cloak dropped over the atrium. Papa Midnight couldn't see his hand in front of his face. Fear clutched at his insides, and the pounding of his heart filled his ears.

"Hello? Hello?" He spoke in the direction of the front desk.

A child giggled, and the hair on the back of his neck stood up. It was so out of place, so lurid, so disturbing, it was a miracle Papa Midnight's bladder didn't empty itself.

He couldn't see, but he sensed the movement all around him. Something brushed past his sweats more than once. He turned left and right, hands floating in front of him. A second giggle joined in. Then another. And another.

"What's happening? Who's there?"

A man's voice whispered in his ear like a lover. "Hello, Papa."

Startled, the old man whirled around, almost losing his balance in the darkness. Arms outstretched, he felt around for something to steady himself on. Heart pounding, he gulped for breath like he'd run a mile.

"Who are you? What's going on!"

"Don't be scared," the man's voice whispered into his other ear. "We just want to talk to you about the Waves."

"You go to hell! Damn delinquents!"

Something brushed against his leg and then his arm. Something touched his butt. He swung around, hands clutching at empty air.

"Stop this! Turn on the damn lights!"

"You heard the man," Timothy commanded, and the grand entryway blazed bright with light.

Papa Midnight blinked several times, his mind not trusting his vision. His arms dropped limp to his sides.

Beyond a three-foot ring around himself, the atrium was filled with people. Much of the crowd was made up of smaller children, kindergarten age and younger, their pale, tiny faces smeared with blood. Their black, soulless eyes stared hungrily at him. Adults were mixed in, some swaying to music the senior couldn't hear. Several women wore Enchanted Castle T-shirts of various colors.

A thin man, as pale as milk, appeared out of the office area behind the front desk. He was licking blood from his talon-like fingers.

"Your concierge tastes like strawberries," Timothy said, sporting a smile a great white shark would be proud of.

Papa Midnight's body sagged, instantly realizing death was here and it wouldn't be drawn out like his wife's.

But he pulled back his slim shoulders and looked the monstrosity straight in its hell pit eyes.

"Do you know who I am?"

Papa Midnight smirked. "I know what you're not." He looked around. "You're just a mad dog running around spreading rabies."

Timothy licked his fingers clean and clapped at the old man's bravado. The senior sensed a subtle surge in the crowd surrounding him. It was as if an invisible leash was keeping each of them at bay.

"You've got some sauce, old man, that's for sure. Before we get to the main course of our visit to the premiere senior living community in the South Bay—as voted by readers of the *Los Angeles Times* in 2019—I have a fun dilemma you might be able to help me with. As you can see, I'm creating an army. Well, actually, let's call it a super gang. But we need a name. You know, something even cooler than the Waves ..." The vampire snorted, amused with himself.

The mob hadn't moved an inch closer, but Papa Midnight felt the heat of their foul breath. "Forget you," he snapped, and then closed his eyes and started reciting the Lord's Prayer.

Timothy moved toward the old man. "I like the lyrics but you can't dance to it."

His jaw yawned wide, like a snake's, and then returned to its normal size. A pair of long fangs slipped out from under his upper lip.

"I wish for your sake this wasn't going to hurt, but where would be the fun in that?" A split second later, Timothy stood behind Papa Midnight, tilting the man's head to the side. The pair of razor-sharp fangs slipped into the man's dark flesh and the man stopped talking. His eyes rolled back into his head, showing only white.

Papa Midnight's body convulsed. A wet stain blossomed on the crotch of his sweatpants, and the unmistakable stench of shit filled the air. Timothy held the man in a grotesque embrace for a few seconds more and then let him crumble to the carpet like the leftover wrapper from a fast-food meal. Timothy stepped over the body, his chest heaving from the process. He dismissively waved a hand, and the closest ring of the surrounding vampire children dove on top of their last meal at the Sunset Dunes.

The majority of the crowd obediently followed their leader to the front entrance and then stopped and awaited his commands. Tangerine had made her way to his side.

"I have one final stop this evening. Complete the mission here and then head back to the sanctuary. I'll join you sometime after midnight." He grinned like a hungry hyena.

Tangerine nodded and then returned inside in search of any scraps. Timothy could hear her frustrated hissing. Those little devils sure could eat.

Next stop—the San Fernando Valley.

11

SAND WORMS

Breeze dropped to the sand, his laughter loud and boisterous. It had been an awesome day so far. After hanging out with the guys at the garage for a while, the group went to the beach to really reconnect with their roots—the surf and the sand. Everyone went, though everyone wasn't going to stick around and accept the twenty-four-hour challenge Bam laid out. But no one seemed to be counting hours or watching the clock. They played some beach volleyball when they first arrived, and then some of the group went surfing while a few lay around on the sand and relaxed. A couple headed up to the outdoor workout area to show off and one-up each other.

Breeze smiled so much he thought his face would crack. He'd forgotten how much fun a day at the beach with the guys was. He'd been a pretty good player back in high school when the Waves rarely left the beach, except to patrol or meet a challenge. Cheyenne had been great, both in the gym and on the sand, which made him work to not look bad when they played together.

Now, away from the beach so much, he could barely hold his own. He watched the best of the bunch pair off and take the sand court. Crater and Sailor took one side while Jim/Joe and Jester ducked under the net to the other side. Breeze watched the first few points, marveling at how

93

quick the thick-bodied Jester was. And despite his heavy musculature, the Samoan could get up at the net too.

The original Wave leader rolled to his back, bunching up a towel for his head. The baking warmth of the sun relaxed Breeze. He dug his toes into the baked sand and the heat cocooned his feet. It reminded him of the summer days when Cheyenne would bury him in the hot sand and he'd fall asleep.

He closed his eyes, and it wasn't long before the surrounding sounds—the guys playing volleyball, random conversation from the passing beachgoers, squeals of playing children, seagulls near and far—all began to fade away like the steam from his wife's favorite hot tea.

He startled awake, choking on cold, foul seawater. He could hardly feel his arms and legs. A strong hand was gripping his arm, tugging frantically. Breeze couldn't make out the face of who it was, and the sound of the ocean masked the person's voice.

"Breeze! Wake up! Wake up, man!" the voice shouted as a wave bobbed Breeze up and down. A large full moon shone high in the night sky, but its reflection was lost on the ocean surface.

"We gotta get to the beach, man!" The man released Breeze's arm and started swimming toward shore like it was an Olympic pool final. Something in the dark water bumped against him, and he swiped his hand over his face to get a clearer look. It was a dead body, but impossible to tell if it was a man or woman. Startled, he looked around himself, and the ocean was full of dead bodies as far as the moonlight allowed him to see. Panicked, he sank under the surface for a few seconds and then pushed away the closest body and started to swim. Breeze tried to follow the path of the lead swimmer, but it wasn't easy. He was an excellent swimmer, but his body felt heavy and stiff like he'd already swum miles in the icy water. He could see the distant outline of the shore, but it was almost as if he was swimming in place.

He was suddenly stumbling through shallow water onto the beach, the dark figure just ahead. It appeared to be a guy, but he still couldn't make out who it was.

"Keep moving," the man shouted. "They're coming!"

Breeze glanced over his shoulder, and he stumbled to a stop. The shoreline was crowded with bodies rising from the ocean and walking into the sand. Their eyes blazed in the darkness like hot coals. As they shambled out of the water, their arms were raised in front of them like Frankenstein. None of them spoke, and the night hid their expressions, but their intention was obvious.

Someone grabbed his arm and almost yanked him off his feet. "Run!"

Breeze did. He almost fell in the loose sand, fighting to get his balance. He got his legs under him, and then he was flying across the sand, feeling like he was seventeen again. The beach might as well have been a premier track. His muscular arms pumped in sync with his powerful legs, and he knew the things from the water would never catch him.

The man who'd led him through the body-laden surf was no longer in front of him. He was gone. Breeze looked as he ran, but the beach was abandoned. He veered toward the lone lifeguard tower. It should have an emergency phone line to the police station. He'd make a call and end this nightmare.

He glanced over his shoulder to check the distance he knew he'd put between himself and the things but was shocked to see the initially slow-moving bodies were now after him at a much faster pace. They weren't running, but they were coming.

"Fuck," he whispered between breaths as he continued his life-or-death sprint.

He was running so fast when he reached the tower he had to grab a support leg to stop himself. He yanked open the phone box as he turned to face the oncoming mob. Their sheer numbers blocked where the water met the beach.

The old-fashioned phone came away in his hand. The cord between the handset and the box had been severed. He threw the phone away and took a moment to evaluate his situation. The far ends of the crowd had begun to swallow up his most direct escape route to the parking lot. He might still make it ... and then a wave of weariness washed over him, his once strong limbs now heavy again. He knew he'd never reach safety no matter which way he ran.

The crowd was closing in, and the reek of dead flesh filled the air. He gagged and ran up the tower's ramp. He thought about going inside the small, single-room shack, but it seemed to make more sense to make his stand in the open air. The narrow ramp would limit the number of things advancing off the sand. He jostled himself, loosening up his arms and shoulders, flexing his fingers into fists. The mass of people filled his vision from the ocean to just yards away. As the first of the dead things approached, he crouched, fists floating in front of his face. He cried out as the first one stumbled up the ramp, growling like a rabid stray.

Breeze stepped toward his attacker and threw a pair of quick jabs. It was enough to throw the man off balance, tumbling backward down the ramp and into the others. Time slowed as the others crawled and stepped over him.

"Come on!" Breeze challenged, focusing on one opponent at a time and not the impossible numbers he could never hope to defeat.

The Wave leader stepped into the second attacker, knocking away his hands and then slamming his elbow across the man's face. He heard a welcome crunch from the man's nose as he pitched off the ramp into the sea of things waiting their turn. He stepped into a front kick, pushing the next one back into the surge at the bottom of the ramp. He dropped the fourth with a crisp left-right combination.

Without thinking, Breeze leapt into a fierce Superman punch, connecting into the next one's jaw and dropping him to the wooden ramp. The punch threw Breeze off balance on the slanted ramp, and as he landed and stumbled toward the faceless mob, he heard a voice speaking to him. He couldn't tell if he heard the man in his ears or if the words were somehow in his mind.

"We're coming for you, Breeze."

He fell into the crowd and was instantly swallowed up. He continued to fight and struggle, but too many tore at him, crushing him by their sheer numbers. He tried to throw a punch but his arms were pinned. Sharp fingernails tore away his clothing and ripped at his flesh. Mouths yawned full of teeth, their whiteness gleaming from their black maws.

"If you can't save yourself, how are you going to save your family and friends?"

The statement was so direct, so personal, Breeze stopped struggling for a moment, shocked by the utter truth of the words.

The murderous sea of things pulled him under, his scream of pain and fear and hopelessness swallowed up as his life was taken by a thousand bites and slashes.

———————

"Breeze?'

A familiar voice was calling his name, even as he struggled against the crush of things.

"Breeze? Wake up, man!"

They were all over him, tearing the flesh from his bones from head to foot. He was dying but couldn't give up—

He got an arm free and snapped off a quick jab.

Jester caught it in his thick-fingered paw inches from his face. Breeze cried out, but it died in his throat a second later. The volleyball-playing Waves surrounded him, Jester and Jim/Joe kneeling on either side. Sailor and Crater stood, blocking the sun.

"You're getting slow," Jester said with an amused smirk.

Breeze exhaled deeply. "Well, I was asleep when I threw it."

Bam came running up. "What's going on?"

"Someone watched a scary movie before bedtime," Crater joked.

"Bad dream," Breeze explained, reaching up.

Bam pulled his leader to his feet. "You all right?"

He shrugged. "Yeah. Just some *Night of the Living Dead* shit. My subconscious working something out."

Breeze glanced toward the Pucker Up Lemonade Stand, and for a split second he thought he saw someone sitting at one of the tables under an umbrella staring at him from behind a pair of sunglasses and a ballcap. He squinted and blinked and the guy was gone.

"We need to get to the Pearls before sunset," Bam reminded.

Breeze nodded. "Gather everyone and let's get gone."

The mini-huddle broke up, leaving Breeze to stare out at the blue surf. The ocean was dotted with swimmers and surfers, not bodies and death. The remnants of his nightmare caused a chill, but he shook it off. Only he felt his bravado. He couldn't remember the last time he had a nightmare. Something was wrong. He needed to finish up this Wave business and get back to his wife and unborn child.

A minor parade of vehicles snaked their way into the parking lot of the Pearls' hangout. Classic hip-hop and R&B music greeted the Waves along with a small crowd and the smell of sizzling barbecue. The Waves fell into formation behind Breeze and Bam as they approached the gathering.

Moon and Crazy Mabel stepped away from the group. Moon's expression morphed from inquisitive hardness to warm and welcoming. She and Breeze stepped to each other, Breeze's body language relaxing.

"Moon."

"Breeze."

The pregnant pause hung in the air like cigar smoke.

"I understand you have something of ours?"

Moon chuckled, and she wasn't alone. "You into sharing your women now? I'm shocked."

A scream came from inside the building. The Pearls mixed throughout the gathering immediately darted inside, Moon and Crazy Mabel right on their heels.

Breeze, Bam, and Crater followed at the front of the Waves. Everyone snaked their way through the building and into the bunk room. A Pearl knelt by the bunk Cheyenne had been resting on. As they got closer, they could see the twin bed was blood spattered. A crumpled body lay on the floor. The young woman's limbs were twisted, and the last of her blood pumped out of her ravaged throat. A lake of her blood was big enough for the deceased to make a grotesque snow angel in. Her wide eyes stared into eternity while her mouth was frozen in a silent cry.

"What the fuck?" Crazy Mabel said, her eyes following a trail of blood up the wall and out a small window well off the floor. Too high for a WNBA player to have jumped and pulled herself out of. But the blood didn't lie.

"I came in to relieve Roberta and found her like this," the rattled Pearl screamer said, looking everywhere but down at the body.

Moon turned on Breeze, snarling. "Your ... bitch ... killed my sister. We did you a fucking favor and look what it cost us!"

Crater and Bam looked at each other.

Breeze addressed his men. "Did you know Cheyenne was dangerous?"

"Dangerous? She was barely conscious," Bam said.

"No way she did this," Crater said.

"If she didn't, who did?" Moon asked. A brooding quiet fell.

"Maybe it wasn't her," Crater said. "Maybe Timothy found her."

"How?" Breeze asked.

"If he can control her like you said, maybe he has some sort of link to her," Crater theorized.

"Makes sense," Bam said.

Breeze looked at the Pearl leader. "We need to call the cops."

Moon shook her head. "We're holding some stuff on property."

"Drugs?"

"Fuck no," Moon answered. "Some electronics fell off a truck. Be outta here first thing Monday morning."

Crazy Mabel took a blanket from a neighboring bunk and covered the dead girl. She looked at the two leaders. "Someone came into our house and butchered one of us. Give the word, Moon." The Pearl leader stared at the body.

"Sweep our territory, but do not engage or hurt her. Am I clear?" There was a smattering of acknowledgement. She looked at Breeze. "We need to be sure who the real killer is."

"You heard Moon," Crazy Mabel rallied. "Pair up and hit the streets." The big woman turned back to her leader.

"I'll take care of Roberta," Moon whispered, kneeling by the corpse, head bowed

Breeze dropped a hand on her shoulder. "Would you like some help?" he whispered.

Moon shook her head and waved him off. "I've got it. I'll call you if she turns up."

"We'll sit on her place in case she goes home," Crater said. "I'll take the volleyballers with me, if that's okay," he asked Breeze.

"Do it," the Wave leader responded. "I have to get back home. If the shit hits the fan, call me."

"What do you call this?" Moon hissed. Breeze didn't have an answer.

"We'll take care of it," Crater said, leading Sailor, Jim/Joe, and Jester back out the way they came.

101

"I'm sorry for this," Breeze said softly and then led the rest of the Waves out. The Wave leader did his best to put the grotesque body out of his mind, along with the mysterious disappearance of Cheyenne. He needed to get home to his very pregnant wife as soon as possible. She wasn't going to believe all the crazy bullshit he had to share.

Breeze already had enough stories to tell from his street gang days.

12

HOME IS WHERE THE HORROR IS

Breeze had just passed the LAX/Century Boulevard exit when his phone went off. It was Bam. He took the call via the minivan's console touch screen.

"What's up?"

"You got the radio on?"

"Nope. Why?"

"Just heard a report involving Sunset Dunes Retirement Community."

"Sunset Dunes ... Wait, where Papa Midnight lives?"

"Yeah. The report says something major happened last night. So far only family members of residents are being notified. I've reached out to someone in the local PD for some info but nothing yet."

"You call Papa?" Breeze asked.

"I tried. No answer at his place or the emergency cell." A big sigh came from the minivan's dashboard. "I'm a little worried, man."

Breeze was quiet. First Stallion, and then Cheyenne, and now possibly Papa Midnight. What the fuck was going on?

"All right. Let me know when you hear something. I'll put the radio on as soon as we get off."

"All right. I'll holler," Bam said and then hung up.

Breeze turned the radio to a news station and then squeezed the steering wheel. The northbound traffic slowed to a crawl. It would stay that way until he reached Mulholland Drive. Saturday night westside traffic. Shit.

Valley Village seemed forever away. Breeze thought about calling Judi but shrugged off the urge. Like he was just thinking, his new home was a world away from all the South Bay craziness.

He listened to the radio long enough to hear a short item about Sunset Dunes and then switched it to a music station. The classic Blue Oyster Cult song "Don't Fear the Reaper" was on.

The dash entertainment screen flashed on, interrupting the music with an incoming call. It was Judi.

"Hi, baby," Breeze said. But the line went dead. He immediately tried her back. It rang and rang. He stared at the dash like it was deliberately screwing with him. His call went to her voicemail.

"Shit." His fingertip brushed the touchscreen to redial. Her cell phone rang. And rang. And rang. Voicemail again.

Breeze stared out the windshield. To his left, the sun was edging toward the horizon. Suddenly the thought of not getting home before dark sent a chill up his spine. He started to press redial but decided against it. It wasn't going to get him home any faster. If it went to her voicemail again it was just going to make him crazy. Everything was fine.

He eased forward a few car lengths and then stopped again. He wasn't even close to the 10 freeway yet. Jesus.

Without thinking, he hit redial. Each ring took his anxiety to a higher level. When her voicemail came on, he forced himself to be calm.

"Hi, honey. It's Wally. I thought you tried to call me a little bit ago. I'm on the way home, but I'm caught up in

Saturday night traffic on the 405. I'm hoping to be home by dark, give or take. Call me, otherwise I'll see you soon. Love you."

He ended the call and stared at the endless bumper-to-bumper traffic. Getting off the freeway onto a major surface street appealed to his impatience, but he knew it wasn't the right thing to do.

The sun was all but down as the traffic eased and the Hollywood 101 exits approached. He couldn't remember how long he'd been holding his breath. The minivan took the 101 South exit toward Hollywood but was greeted with more bumper-to-bumper traffic. He cursed and took the first exit. He'd take surface streets home from there.

Judi never called him back. He didn't want to make her nervous by calling her again.

A call came through. Not Judi. Bam.

"Dude, what's up?" He couldn't stop his frustration from leaking through.

Bam cleared his throat. "My contact at the police department says the Sunset Dunes community is a hot wet mess. Dead bodies everywhere. A bunch of staff and residents are missing."

"What? What are you talking about?"

"Papa Midnight was found dead by the front desk by the main entrance. He'd been torn to pieces."

"Jesus." Breeze exhaled. He accelerated the minivan through a yellow light. He was less than ten minutes from home.

"Breeze, we just had breakfast. He was going to help."

"Can't be a coincidence." Breeze searched his mind for any reasonable explanations. There weren't any.

"And no word about Cheyenne?"

"Nada."

"Hey, I'm just about home. I'll call you back in a bit," Breeze said.

"Later," Bam replied and hung up.

The siren from an LAPD patrol car blared as it streaked past, startling Breeze. He grew closer and closer to home by the block. The police car seemed to be headed in the same direction. A second police car joined just a few blocks from his house. Breeze fought back the anxiety and stayed focused on his destination.

The police cars stopped a block from his house, their roof berry lights flashing in the early evening shadows.

Breeze didn't slow as he cruised down that last block and swung the minivan into the wide driveway, parking directly behind Judi's small SUV. The house was dark with the exception of the small automatic porch light. The garage door was down.

He glanced up the street. The incident had drawn multiple police vehicles. He jogged up to the front door. He fumbled the house keys in his hand. He shouldn't be this anxious. Everything was fine.

He bounced onto the porch. When he inserted the master key, the front door pushed open. The interior of the house was dark. His free hand balled into a fist.

"Judi?" he called out, hesitant as he stepped across the threshold. There was no reply.

He reached in and flipped the entryway light switch. Nothing came on.

"Judi?" he said again.

A faint sound from the master bedroom. He cut through the living room and moved down the hallway. He clinched his keyring in his other fist.

"Wally?" A whisper of a woman's voice barely reached him.

"Honey?" he responded, stepping into their bedroom. The room was dark, but a sliver of light leaked around the edge of the bathroom door. The glow wavered and danced.

Candles. Judi loved taking a hot bath with her scented candles. Ocean breeze was her favorite. Of course it was. His anxiety began to evaporate.

"Judi, you okay?"

"I'm fine, Wally. I nodded off taking a bath." He started across the room but she stopped him. "Don't come in. Let me finish up."

A nervous smile flirted across his lips. Judi had been feeling unattractive for the last few weeks, so he wasn't surprised. He flipped the bedroom light switch but nothing happened. She spoke up again as if she had X-ray vision.

"I think we blew a fuse, so we probably don't have any lights."

"Gotcha," he answered, sitting on the edge of their Cal king bed. It was the first thing they'd bought once the house was theirs. He'd grown up sleeping on a twin bed, so it felt weird to have so much room, considering they slept against each other most every night. Her quiet snoring was like a lullaby.

"I'll be done in a minute. Just sit and chat with me. I missed you today."

"I missed you too."

"How was everyone?"

"Everyone was good. I think I was the longshot to show." He chuckled at the truth. "Everyone said to tell you hello."

"Even Joe?" The question caught Breeze off guard. Jim/Joe had always made her feel uncomfortable. Paranormal stuff was not her thing.

"Not sure about Joe," he answered, "though I suppose he was there."

"A friend of yours stopped by while you were gone. Said he knew you from high school."

Breeze looked at the bathroom door, suddenly uneasy. "Someone stopped by?"

"Uh huh. He was very nice. Didn't want to come in when I told him you weren't here."

Before Breeze could respond, a low, odd noise came from the bathroom, and then she continued. "Did you remember my driftwood?"

Breeze grimaced. He'd forgotten. "I'm sorry, sweetie. I totally forgot. I'll call Sailor and see if he can gather some for you, and I'll grab it up next trip."

Judi didn't respond. A few seconds passed.

Judi's voice was barely a whisper through the door. "He said you didn't love me. That you never really loved me."

Breeze wasn't sure he'd heard her right. "What'd you say, honey?"

"He said your heart would always belong to Cheyenne and the water, child or no child. Marriage or no marriage ..."

Breeze got up from the bed and started toward the bathroom door. "That's not true. Who said that?"

He heard Judi moan as his hand grasped the bathroom doorknob.

"Don't come in," Judi ordered. His hand froze on the knob.

"What's happening?" Breeze's voice didn't come out as strong as he thought it would. A cold fear sat like a frozen seed waiting to blossom in his gut. He was suddenly afraid of the doorknob. He was afraid to turn it and afraid to let it go. It had been one of the smaller details Judi loved about their home.

"What are you doing?" His whisper was louder than he wanted. He didn't want to ask the question and knew he didn't want to know the answer. A slithering kind of fear he never knew existed uncoiled in the deepest part of his gut.

A stark silence filled the room. Breeze stared at his hand and the knob. The uncertainty was paralyzing. Half a minute stretched into a full minute. He was holding his breath, waiting for her, for something. His eyes began to moisten, and the slightest tremble invaded the hand on the knob.

"We were going to be a family," she finally whispered back, her voice as quiet and weak as a dying baby bird.

The knob was turning before he fully realized it. He heard his wife mumbling as he stepped into the steam from the claw-footed shower tub. It was bright in the bathroom, so he couldn't miss the bloody carving knife on the floor beside the tub. His wife was in the tub, the water right to the edge, dark red with blood. Head leaned back, her eyes were closed. She gripped the edges of the tub, her slashed wrists still oozing blood into the water. Her midsection had been carved open from sternum to navel. A small, unmoving form floated by her kneecaps.

Breeze sank to his knees, tears streaming down his face. He was still holding on to the doorknob like it was a lifeline. Was that his little boy floating face down? His little girl lifeless in the red-stained water? The white-hot agony of the moment branded the image onto his soul. They hadn't even decided on names yet. *Oh my God.*

He watched the water slowly swallow his dead wife's face.

He jerked his eyes away. The blood-smeared message on the medicine cabinet mirror caught his attention.

SEE YOU SOON

The note looked crude, scrawled by a finger. Breeze retched at the thought of someone dipping their finger into his wife's blood. It was an invasion he would not forget. Or forgive.

He was screaming as he fumbled with his cell phone, his hands and fingers shaking too badly to press 911. He threw the phone against the wall in frustration, shattering the device. He staggered back through the house, half falling over furniture between the darkness and his tear-blurred eyes. Breeze fell out the front door, still screaming as he moved toward the police lights.

Everything else, for a while, became an ugly, blood-stained blur.

Uniformed and plain-clothes officers spoke to him as he sat outside the front door. The drone of their voices was like a dull dentist drill teasing at an exposed nerve. An ex offensive lineman stuffed into a police uniform was posted by his side. Despite his innocence, he understood he was a suspect until they discovered proof he wasn't. He wasn't sure what that would be.

Multiple officers had to restrain him as the EMTs pushed the gurneys past him, the sheet-wrapped bodies of his family taunting him. The gurney with his dead child almost appeared empty, but a second glance showed the tiny bundle near the head of the stretcher, the sheet spattered in dark blood. Even though he'd been speaking to Judi moments before her death, he hadn't said goodbye to her. Now gone forever, he couldn't remember the last words he'd said to her. It should have been I love you, but he knew that it wasn't.

13

PULLING THE WINGS OFF FLIES

Timothy stood on the roof of the building across from the long-shuttered Bastion Theater. It sat in the middle of the soon-to-be-revitalized area of downtown Pacific Grove, an eight-block section of older brick buildings, abandoned retail stores, and manufacturing establishments not suited for individual resurrection. Timothy looked around from his vantage point. The new Grove Center, a massive retail, entertainment, and urban living community was set to break ground six months ago. Historical preservation groups got involved when the project price tag became astronomical and more land was required. The Grove Center was a key political topic in an election year. So the empty buildings sat patiently awaiting their evolution.

Timothy looked at the Bastion Theater, and a flood of memories washed through his mind. His parents were big movie fans, and he spent many a summer Saturday morning watching something fun with his family. Its screen was the largest in the area, only behind a couple in Hollywood.

The area was quiet outside of the few wandering stray animals. The homeless had long since been herded out, and private security held a minimal presence in the area, but nothing to concern the Master. He'd secured his surroundings shortly after he'd chosen the Bastion for his lair. A private patrol car sat in front of the theater.

With only a stray cat as a witness, Timothy reached over the edge of the building and scurried down the rough brick surface like a cockroach. He dropped to the sidewalk seconds later, frightening the cat into the shadows. He strolled across the street, casually passing in front of the security car. The uniformed man behind the wheel ignored Timothy despite his head being on a constant swivel. Timothy pushed through the unlocked front glass doors.

Like so many grand, single-screen theaters, the Bastion was once the centerpiece of its downtown community. Catering to everyone regardless of age, race, or social position, the Bastion planted lasting memories— great films, first dates, first kisses, the dark, inviting back row of the balcony ...

And then came the multiplex theaters.

The Bastion held up better than most, but business eventually began to wane. Ownership began to hot potato, the huge single screen was split in half, and then quarters. Timothy moved through the dark, dust-layered lobby, the empty poster frames watching him like sightless eyes. The long-abandoned concession stand was filled with cobwebs and more dead spiders than live ones.

Timothy's evolution included night vision, the world tinted in vivid crimson. He paused at the junction of the left balcony staircase and the curtained entrance into the theater's lower main seating. He loved the view from up high.

He had great memories of growing up in that theater. Family movie nights where his dad would buy a giant tub of hot buttered popcorn and they would pass it back and forth, pausing with each kid just long enough for them to grab a handful. He sometimes shared with his baby sister, whose little hands couldn't hold much. His parents worked hard at the deli, and Timothy loved watching his mother and father laugh through the comedies and squint through their fingers during the scary movies.

He pushed through the heavy velvet curtains. The Master's army was filling up the theater's main section and stage. The place was strangely quiet outside of the hushed shuffling of some of the newer converts, whose evolution made it hard to be still. As he got closer to the stage, Timothy could hear music leaking up from the storage cellar below. It was from the seventies. His dad loved the music from that decade. Timothy recognized the song but didn't know the words. The Master seemed to know the words to every song.

At the rear of the stage, behind the movie screen, he pulled open a wooden trapdoor and descended a narrow set of stairs. The music was blaring, made deafening by Timothy's heightened hearing. The high-pitched whine of the electric guitar made him wince. That song ended and another began as he stepped into the Master's dimly lit chambers. It was one of his dad's favorites to sing along with, Steppenwolf's "Hey Lawdy Mama." Timothy always thought it was a weird name. His father used to sing it in the car all the time. When he was little he used to laugh at his dad as he really got into the drums and air guitar, but it wasn't until he got a little older that Timothy began to understand the power of music, and how a song could mark special moments in your life.

The Master giggled and then his voice warbled badly out of tune. "I like to dream, yeah, yeah ..."

The stench of sex, bad body odor, and an unflushed toilet struck Timothy like an open-handed slap. He should

114

have been used to it by now, yet every visit seemed to reveal a new foul fragrance. Timothy recognized the sickly-sweet poison as his own leaking from Cheyenne's festering thigh wound. She was curled up on the bare concrete floor like a wounded animal. Rivulets of sweat made streaks across her dirty skin. Eyes closed, she shivered from the infection's fever.

Across the room, the Master was relaxing in a wide, black leather loveseat recliner, his black satin robe splayed open. The head of the pretty receptionist from the daycare was lost in his fleshy lap. The Master's head was thrown back in pleasure.

Timothy stopped just inside the room, his attention torn between his love and the source of his new power.

Half a minute passed and the Master moaned, his hips grinding against the young woman's face. His hands, like owl talons, reached down and burrowed into her hair, trapping her until he finished. The woman's body language signaled panic as she tried to pull away. Her fingernails dug into the Master's flabby thighs, but he ignored her desperation as his climax neared. Timothy wasn't sure if the Master's razor-sharp nails had only grabbed hair or had sunk into the woman's skull. Timothy winced at the merciless onslaught. He knew the Master was the ultimate apex predator, not to be denied in any of his wants or needs.

The Master roared like a lion as he reached his climax, his chins quivering like Jello. The Enchanted Castle Preschool receptionist, choking, suffocating, or both, was frantically struggling to escape his clutches, but his strength was overwhelming despite the fact the spirit of the master vampire was housed in the obese body of a fourteen-year-old boy named Jerrod Leach.

Finishing, he grunted with each violent hip thrust. He collapsed into his loveseat recliner, discarding the young woman as if she'd been a handful of Kleenex.

"Do not let one drop touch the floor," he commanded.

She fell to the floor, careful to keep her mouth closed tight until she'd swallowed it. Then she gasped for air as she spider-crawled across the room to the farthest corner, as if being close to Cheyenne would shield her from future abuse. Her eyes were wide with fear and disgust.

Eyes closed to the world, Jerrod Leach purred with contentment. "I could control her mind, make her accept the whore she is, but the very best control is fear. Fear of the consequences if you're not obeyed. Remember that."

Timothy nodded. It was weird obeying an obese teenager, but he kept reminding himself that the Master was really almost one hundred years old.

Timothy's head was full of bits and pieces about the Master. During the process of his evolution, some of the Master's memories were passed on to him. As if the Master was a book, Timothy got glances of words and phrases, glimpses of images associated with them. He'd seen the Master as a young man in pre-WWII Germany. His father had been a chef. His beautiful mother had raised him but spent mysterious evenings absent from their home. At some point his father had left the house, and his mother's evenings out now extended through the night. A neighbor woman was assigned to watch him on the nights his mother was out. The details were vague, but it was the neighbor's daughter Helga who'd made Jerrod a vampire. Since Timothy's evolution, his mind was sometimes invaded by the Master's fever dreams of their torrid teenage affair. Timothy couldn't help but be aroused by the vivid acts and images.

116

Timothy had gotten used to the vampire's casual nudity but was careful about making lingering or aggressive eye contact with the Master. He didn't take kindly to perceived challenges from his minions.

"Good evening," the Master greeted, still basking in the glow of his orgasm.

Timothy bent to a knee then and stood back up. "Master."

"You've done an excellent job creating my army," the Master congratulated in his high voice.

The compliment made Timothy feel uncomfortable. Kindness wasn't the Master's way. Timothy glanced at Cheyenne, who was curled up on the floor like a dog. She might have been sleeping. The woman from the daycare was right next to her.

"Thank you for taking care of her." As soon as the words left his mouth, Timothy knew he'd made a mistake.

The Master's head snapped forward, and his gold snake eyes glared. "Don't forget your place. If I want her, I'll take her. I'll have her ground up into sausages, or I'll take her head off her shoulders, eat her eyes, and fuck the empty sockets. Understand?"

Timothy simply nodded, afraid to make any verbal response.

"In time you'll learn that love is as real as the boogeyman. Urges can be satisfied in countless ways and with countless girls."

Timothy nodded again, thankful the Master seemed to be calming down.

"You take care of your personal errand in the Valley?"

Timothy couldn't stop a grin from growing. "I did. Everything went perfectly."

The Master raised an eyebrow. "So the great Wallace Thornton won't be sitting out our invasion of the South Bay?"

"Definitely not. He will be extremely motivated to seek revenge."

The Master licked his thick tongue across his lips. "Revenge tastes so sweet in the blood. Like cinnamon."

"I look forward to watching you feed from his broken body."

"You continue not to disappoint me and you'll be rewarded for your service."

Timothy stole a peek at his desire.

The Master sighed. "Oh. As you wish, you poor devil."

Timothy's grin grew into a toothy smile. He crossed the room, causing the woman from the daycare to mew like a scared kitten. As he knelt, his snarl caused the woman to crawl away. He gently grasped Cheyenne's shoulder and turned her onto her back. A grubby, faded lemon-colored sweatshirt covered her upper body, but the matching sweatpants were long disposed of. Her tanned, shapely legs were hard to ignore. He reached between her thighs and spread her legs. She moaned, half-conscious. He grew half-hard just looking at the healing bite mark on her inner thigh. Timothy's mouth watered as he moved in to feed. He could hear the daycare woman whispering a prayer.

"Stop your sniveling!" The Master shouted and then ripped off a loud, squealing fart that might not have been just toxic gas. The fumes reached Timothy as his fangs sank into Cheyenne's flesh. Her back arched from the floor at the penetration. His eyes showed white as they rolled up into his head, high on what he was taking from and giving to her. Her fingers found his head and held it with the strength of a scoring addict.

118

Across the room, Jerrod Leach's nose wrinkled at the stench from the mess he made of himself. He snapped his fingers in the direction of the daycare receptionist. "You. Go into the theater and fetch me several toddlers. I need cleaning up."

The woman cowered, whimpering at his attention.

"Now!" he screamed, startling Timothy to the point of disengaging.

The woman yelped and sprinted for the door as if his voice had set her aflame.

"I like the tongues of little ones," the Master said to no one in particular. "They're not all sandpapery like a cat's."

14

FANGS FOR THE MEMORIES

Timothy's voice was like a cool, slippery-smooth snake slithering in her head. It was impossible to ignore, forcing any of her personal thoughts into a muted background. Its power reverberated on many levels. Its tone both relaxed and excited her, and it also embedded itself like a fishhook into her subconscious will. It also seemed to act as a perfect distraction as his fangs violated her flesh.

"Think about a happy memory," he instructed as his lips formed a seal against her skin. She gasped and then grunted at the orgasmic sensation of him sucking her blood. It was impossible to keep her hips still as he fed and her mind relived the first time she and Breeze were intimate.

It always felt like summertime in Southern California. Living in a beach community only enforced that feeling. But it was actually early January, and the Christmas break was close to an end. A minor heat wave had hit LA, but the Pacific Ocean had taken the edge off, as usual. Breeze was still Wally to her—more than the gang name that grew to be even what his parents soon called him. The legend of the Waves had yet to happen.

She and Wally were inseparable during the holidays. They practically lived at the beach, with her constantly playing volleyball pickup games. She loved to play, and Wally and his friends loved watching her talent dominate. The other attractive beach bunnies didn't hurt the scene either. It was funny how she'd never felt threatened or jealous of the prettier girls. She'd always felt so secure, and Wally was a bigger fan than her parents. Rumors were USC and UCLA would offer her a full-ride volleyball scholarship. She dreamed of going to USC and of getting a chance to try out for the 2020 Olympics in Tokyo. She'd cram as much school into her scholarship as she could to take the edge off her medical school debt. She'd be a doctor with her own small practice, and Wally would restore old cars, and they'd get married and start a family.

Little details about him haunted her throughout those magical days and nights. She was mesmerized by his lips. She constantly wanted to kiss him. He'd kiss her on her bare shoulder at the beach volleyball courts before rubbing suntan lotion on her, and an electric charge would surge through her body. It had started a pulse between her legs she'd never felt before. Beach showers were lasting longer and longer as the lingering sensations of his tender caresses played across her skin, making her feel crazy, unable to extinguish the searing passion they were igniting.

It was the simplest, most casual details. When they walked down by the water, they rarely held hands. Wally would slip a finger through the middle loop of her cutoffs and press his hand into the small of her back. It felt good with his strong hand just above her butt, which he constantly complimented her about. The positions and rigors of playing the sport made for strong and curvy lower bodies.

Wally often whispered in her ear, making sure his mouth lightly brushed against her skin. At first it tickled, but soon it grew into a very private way for them to touch without causing their parents to trip out about birth control and unwanted pregnancies.

Cheyenne had watched him grow into his body with a fascination and growing hunger. Despite not playing sports in high school, his work after school at his father's auto repair shop was adding muscles as his height sprouted beyond their eye-to-eye challenges. As he'd gotten a little older, his father had allowed him to let his hair grow to his broadening shoulders. The female population of Pacific Grove High School was taking notice too. Rumors stirred of more than one woman teacher and younger single mothers of his classmates appreciating his looks. But it wasn't merely his looks. There were other handsome guys among the student body. Even among the Wave membership, Stallion couldn't bend over to tie his shoes without some girl staring or whispering a comment. Surgeon was great looking too. But Wally had those little intangibles that made him special. He was popular but without the aid of being a jock, or having a family with money, or being creatively talented. Adults liked him.

He was as cool as shit without trying to be. And he belonged to her.

It was the Saturday evening before they returned to school on Monday morning. After she'd finished playing at the beach, they'd hung out with the guys down at the Pacific Grove pier. They'd had fun at the arcade, and he'd had her nerves jangling when they'd played her favorite pinball machine. She grew up watching her parents play an older version, and her mom and dad laughed and enjoyed themselves, sometimes taking turns but mostly playing together, her dad standing close behind her mom. Sometimes her father whispered something too quiet for her and her sister to hear, but it would always make her mom smile or laugh and sometimes made her blush. She'd playfully discourage him, but he'd kiss her on the cheek or sometimes pat her bottom.

Now she'd tell her parents about being at the arcade with Wally playing pinball, and they'd glance at each other, sharing a knowing look. Cheyenne was certain they had no idea how he made her feel when he stood behind her, leaning against her as they played. She loved the feel of his body against hers, the hint of mint from his breath across her cheek. Sometimes they'd get into such a great run she'd almost not notice her bottom pushing back into his groin, and him sometimes bumping back against her.

Almost.

That Saturday evening, as guys casually drifted away to attend to their own evenings, Cheyenne watched him destroy a crunchy corn dog from Moon Doggie's, and decided she was going to fuck him that night. They weren't going to make love like in the movies, and he wasn't going to fuck her like in the couple of porno movies she'd explored with her friends. No, she was going to fuck him and end all the hopes and dreams of all the other girls and women of world and make Wallace "Breeze" Thornton, the coolest grease monkey in the world, hers forever. She'd gone to the bathroom and checked her small backpack. At the bottom was a condom her best friend, Connie, had slipped her shortly after she and Wally had started going out. The early rep of the Waves was much more as make-out kings than fighters, something Stallion was more than happy to maintain.

The sun had all but disappeared under the horizon, and she asked Wally to walk with her down by the water. Of course he agreed, and he slipped his hand onto her

123

lower back as usual. She walked them just out to the reach of the pier's amusement ride lighting when she turned into him and kissed him. That kiss sparked a flame that quickly engulfed them both.

She asked him if he wanted to go under the pier, and he said he'd go wherever she wanted. She led him, their fingers tightly intertwined. The underneath portion of the pier was fenced off, but there were holes and gaps and they found one and slipped into the cool darkness. She had a tiny light on her keyring, and they found a spot in the sand. The sound of the surf mixed with the mechanical noises of the amusement park rides above them, and she could barely hear him. They kissed and touched in a passionate rush, clothing getting shed as it impaired their inspired exploration. When his fingers slid over the damp crotch of her panties, her body reacted so strongly he paused and asked if she was okay. She smiled and laughed, assuring him with her tongue down his throat that she was just fine. When his fingers slipped under the waistband of her underwear, she broke off their deep kiss and bit him on his earlobe and whispered what she wanted. The darkness robbed her from seeing what must have been a comical expression on his face as he asked if he'd heard her right. Deciding that wanting him inside her was a bit too fluffy, her next response had used the F-word so there'd be no confusion. One of the strongest details from her memory was his odd hesitation.

And then she suddenly realized something they'd never talked about. Breeze was a virgin and was totally unprepared for this situation. And that made it perfect.

Lost in the memory as if it was happening all over again, Cheyenne's body responded like it had those years back. Feeling his throbbing hardness as she unrolled the condom down his jutting length was one of the sexiest things she'd ever experienced. His breathing was a hushed pant, and his heart was pounding. He'd moved between her legs, and after a fumbling attempt on his part, she'd shushed him like a baby and kissed him softly as she guided him inside her.

The power she felt in that moment almost made her cum.

Wally didn't need much direction. He started slowly, tentative in his movements, but her primal urging melted away his anxiousness. She raised her hips and locked her legs around his hips and very much enjoyed his first effort. When it became clear he was nearing his time, she pulled his face to hers and tried hard to imagine his expression as he came. Their mouths and tongues pressed hard as he strained at his climax, his hips bucking and grinding, nature driving him to penetrate as deeply as possible as her short nails marked the flesh of his shoulder. She didn't have an orgasm, but she'd never made herself feel this good with her fingers in the shower. Never.

Wally had slumped beside her, slipping out of her, his spent member resting along her thigh. She turned on her side and kissed him softly, over and over, delighting as his heaving chest eased to normal. She'd asked him if it had been good and he turned his head and looked at her, finally laughing and saying it was way better than Mama Italy's stuffed slices. The statement made her laugh; it was the perfect cherry to top off their union. He asked her if that meant she was his girlfriend and she'd rabbit punched him in the stomach. He'd grabbed her and they'd wrestled around, laughing until that primal urge reared and their passion ignited again...

Cheyenne's fingers clenched into fists and she came, Timothy's mouth clamped to her inner thigh as her body strained and twisted. The vampire seemed oblivious to her release, totally absorbed in its feeding.

The memory neared its end. She remembered their hunger the second time around didn't feel like a pot of boiling water spilling over. It was a wanton ache for more. There was always room for something so wonderfully good.

Cheyenne grunted and opened her eyes, staring out, as if trying to force her imagination into reality...

She'd only had one condom, the wrapper worn from the contents of her purse. Its condition didn't make them pause, much less stop. She broke off their kissing and flipped onto her stomach. She spread her legs and arched her back to make it easier for him. Wally found his target and slid into her as far as he could go. The surf was loud, but it couldn't completely drown out her moan of pleasure. Fingers clawing into the sand, between breaths she told him to go slow, knowing it would make him crazy.

He hissed okay, and she wallowed in her control, which was just as potent as their coupling. It wasn't hard to determine Wally was straining to do as he was asked, and without thinking, Cheyenne's hand snaked under her belly and down between her legs. Her hips bucked as her fingers found her swollen mound. That movement spurred Wally on, and slow was thrown out the window. Propped above her, his hips moved on their own, forcing him in and out of her with reckless abandon. She remembered the fireworks that exploded from her center, and she bumped herself back at him over and over and her pleasure spilled over and rippled and rippled and rippled …

Wally cried out and grabbed her hips, and she'd cried out for him not to cum inside her. And like the hero he was set to become, Wally ignored the compelling thrust of nature and jerked himself out of her and fell back in the sand, his hardness a dark shadow among other dark shadows. She flipped around and grabbed for him, finding him, squeezing him, and then pumping him. Her sand-covered hand didn't slide up and down his length a half dozen times before he came, his hot semen coating her fingers. He grunted and groaned, almost as if he was hurt, but she knew better and continued to stroke him until he stopped thrusting and relaxed into the sand. When she finally released him, she held up her hand, feeling but wanting to see his sticky gift to her. She had an urge to lick her fingers like they were covered in frosting but she didn't. She'd seen a slutty-looking woman in one of the pornos do that, but Cheyenne didn't want to ruin everything by acting like a slut. She was so happy she laughed out loud. She was a slut, if a slut was a girl who enjoyed sex with her boyfriend. Fuck the world for knowing the truth about her.

Wally sat up and fumbled for her in the darkness. She found his arms and squeezed into them, her skin suddenly covered in goosebumps. They got dressed and escaped the pier fencing. Her backpack slung over her shoulder, she carried her flip flops in the crook of a finger. Wally took her hand, laced his fingers in hers, and gave her a squeeze. They smiled at each other and started back up to the pier. She felt words wanting to come out, but she stayed quiet because Wally did.

Cheyenne smiled with the memory. She'd taken Breeze's virginity, and it had solidified their budding relationship.

On the verge of a second climax, she closed her eyes and waited for the pleasure to overpower her. As it did, she couldn't help herself. "Wally," she whispered as she came, and the memory faded to black.

Timothy's ears perked up at Cheyenne's whisper. He forced his vampiric greed down and finished his feeding, unable to look away from her satisfied expression. The reality of his control over her pierced his ebbing sense of humanity. He was using her feelings for Breeze to control her, but it was also reinforcing that love instead of her drawing closer to him.

Timothy watched her lapse back into a resting semiconsciousness, her simple smile radiating a childlike joy. His jealousy flared, but it didn't become the inferno it might have days before. He snarled at his tactical mistake, unable to shake the Master's advice regarding his soon-to-be-eroded humanity. His love for Cheyenne could no longer continue to drive his thought processes. He clung to the energy that drove his human life, but he had to adapt to his evolution. But while he still had a beating heart, a key thought remained, and Timothy guarded it with his life.

Maybe the Master was wrong.

Maybe a vampire could still love.

15

A FIELD OF DEAD ROSES

Timothy had experienced his share of death and hard times in his relatively short life. The death of his grandmother when he was a young boy was his first real emotional hardship. The wasting away of his mother from brain cancer, and the subsequent drowning death of his father. It was ruled an accidental death, but Timothy knew his father's love of life dissolved when his wife was lowered into the ground after her long, losing battle. His will to live got buried that day too. Less than a month later he took his usual daybreak ocean swim. It was his favorite way to meet his workday. That day, authorities theorized, his father swam a little further out and suffered a minor stroke, causing him to drown. It happened to men his age. They feel good on a particular morning and push their limits and then bam, the old ticker doesn't hold up. A simple case. Open and shut.

Timothy knew his father was more than capable of his routine swim, but it covered up what Timothy knew in his heart. His father couldn't live without his wife of three decades. Didn't want to live without her. Timothy wondered if his father's grief had clouded his thinking. As a devout Catholic, committing suicide was a one-way trip to hell. Publicly he mourned his father's unfortunate loss, but when he was alone he prayed to God to understand his father's loss and to make an exception to allow him to join Timothy's mother in heaven. But at his core, he knew God didn't allow passes to one of his most sacred rules. Timothy understood feeling a love so overpowering a man would give his soul to be with her. Whenever he died as a soulless creature, at least he'd see his father again, even if it was in hell.

Timothy has seen some awful things, but none as bad as the atrocities he'd witnessed these last several days. Right now, he sat across from the Master, his eyes wandering and touching on every detail and item in the room, except the perversions directly across from him.

The Master lounged back in his black leather loveseat lounger, naked as a newborn as a group of toddlers licked him clean from his forehead to the soles of his pasty, overripe feet. The Master's satisfied purring was as nauseating as the sight itself.

Timothy silently cursed his remaining humanity, which allowed him to still feel the complete wrongness of the act, but in these moments he welcomed the growing void where his conscience and morality once lived. No doughy fold of fat was neglected, the children following his commands like worker ants attending to their queen.

Timothy stared at the floor or the web-strewn ceiling when particular areas of the Master's body were licked clean. He told himself that Cheyenne was worth any cruelty the Master could devise and inflict. It was all a test of his devotion to her. The Bible was full of hellish challenges for ordinary men to overcome. Lord knew Timothy was as ordinary as anyone until this last week.

The seconds dragged on like aspirin going down your throat. How much longer could this continue?

The Master suddenly sat up and snapped his sausage fingers. All the kids stopped and peered into his face, awaiting his next order. Timothy closed his eyes in gratitude.

"Enough," the Master said, and the children climbed off. They stood around, not sure what to do.

"Bedtime," the Master said with a single resounding clap. He yawned and stretched and scratched up and down his generous girth. The children fell into an orderly single file and left the room, headed back to the theater. Timothy felt the full weight of the Master's declaration, and he knew its call was irresistible. He felt the weight of his limbs increase, and his thoughts became fuzzy. It was hard to focus, and he lay next to Cheyenne, draping his arm across as his body spooned hers.

The last child turned off the lights and the music. Timothy felt a heavy, absolute black curtain dropping over his consciousness. One last second he was awake, though barely, and then next, he was … gone.

It felt different than regular sleep. It was more of a recharging. It tended to happen at daybreak since nights were a more comfortable time to hunt and feed. Timothy never remembered dreaming, and each sleep was remarkably like the one before. Within an hour of sunset Timothy would wake up. He never felt drowsy or foggy headed or in need of more sleep, like in his old life. He awoke ready to go, fresh in body and mind.

The inky darkness of the Master's chamber might have been soothing had it not been for the accompanying stench and uncomfortable heat. An absence of windows and vents meant no circulating air but worked best for security concerns.

Cheyenne laid on the rough cement floor, her mind floating in and out of consciousness. Sometimes she didn't feel alone, like she was a member of a litter. There were times she swore there was movement in the surrounding darkness. She couldn't have seen her hand right in front of her face, but her hearing was still good. But that was if she was truly awake and not dreaming. Ever since this nightmare began, she didn't know what day it was, much less night or day. At times she was starving, like restaurant dumpster-diving levels, and other times she was so fucking horny she just needed something... inside her. She couldn't remember the last time she went to the bathroom, or changed her clothes, or ate something with a fork. She was so screwed up. Maybe one of her tricks had dropped something in her drink when she wasn't paying attention. She tried hard to be careful, especially with strangers, but even the most experienced professional screwed up.

Wait—

She remembered the night with Stallion - at least pieces of it. That was real. It happened right in front of her eyes.

Something moved in the darkness. At least she thought so.

Stallion was dead. Timothy.

Timothy. The deli guy from her neighborhood. Flashes of him blurred through her mind. She had trouble grasping any of them. Trying to remember anything was hurting her head, so she opened her eyes to the same darkness inhabiting her closed eyes. Maybe it was night.

Maybe she was dead. Oh, God ...

A single flame suddenly blazed inches from her face. She winced, thinking she was dead and in hell.

In the gloom beyond the flame, a woman appeared. She appeared to be Asian, with a dirty face. Her eyes were wide and wild. Her breath reeked of sour milk with a splash of semen.

"Wake up! Wake up!" Her whisper was a desperate plea. She shook Cheyenne's shoulder. Cheyenne whined at the unwelcome intrusion.

"Wake up! We gotta go while they're asleep! The fat one is crazy!"

Cheyenne tried to push the cigarette lighter away. "Go away. Leave me alone."

"If I leave you here, you'll die, or worse, become one of them. I think they're, they're vampires, or something. It's hard to think." She yelped and the flame went out.

Cheyenne closed her eyes. The flame returned a second later. She couldn't ignore it.

"What they did … to the children. It was horrible. He bit me and then made me watch."

Cheyenne saw the pain in the woman's expression and her struggle to keep her composure. She was getting harder to ignore. Her vision swam in and out of focus, but when she saw the ugly puncture marks on the woman's neck, everything became clear.

"We have to go. Now!"

She felt the weight of Timothy's arm draped over her hip, but the woman took it by the wrist and dropped it to the floor. Cheyenne looked back over her shoulder, sure Timothy was going to wake up.

He stared at her through the dim light. He didn't blink, nor did he smile or snarl or bare his fangs.

She jolted but the woman shushed her. "They all sleep like that, with their eyes open. Creepy as hell. But they're all dead to the world as long as the Master guy stays asleep. Come on."

The receptionist grabbed her purse and frantically dug around in it. Cheyenne watched, not really caring enough to ask.

"My name is Kym, by the way. Here." She pulled out her keyring and pushed it into Cheyenne's hand. "Use the flashlight. It's going to be pitch black until we get outside. It should be pretty close to dawn."

Kym pulled her to her feet, but her legs weren't steady. Kym grabbed at her T-shirt to steady her.

"I can't carry you. If you want to live you have to walk."

Kym started toward the room's only door. The lighter's illumination wasn't much, but it was a blessing neither woman could see the Master's wide-eyed stare.

They crept from the room, trying to move as quietly as possible. Cheyenne struggled from the earlier feeding, her limbs feeling heavy. She labored at walking a straight path. They crossed the smaller, adjoining chamber and Kym started up the ladder-like set of stairs, careful not to drop the lighter. She paused at the wooden hatch that led to the theater's stage. She looked down, but her fellow prisoner was still standing at the ladder's base. The little flashlight was pointed at the dusty floor. She was fighting to stay on her feet.

"What are you doing? Come on."

Cheyenne had trouble keeping her head up as she shook it. "I can't do this."

"Fuck," Kym cursed in a hush, She backed down the ladder and took the flashlight from Cheyenne's hand. Her fingers barely held it. Kym helped her with her first steps.

"You can do this," Kym encouraged. "Once we're outside, we'll get help."

Cheyenne whined but kept going. Kim climbed right behind her. When she finally reached the hatch, she shoved at it in anxious desperation, but Kym couldn't do anything to help. The square wooden door banged against the stage floor, echoing through the theater's dead air like a gunshot.

"Shit!" Kym hissed at the sudden noise, fumbling and dropping the lighter. Darkness swallowed them whole.

"I thought ... I thought you said everyone was dead asleep."

Kym nodded, reminding herself. "You're right. I just figured we wouldn't take any chances." Kym switched on the tiny flashlight and passed it to Cheyenne. "Here. Take a peek."

Cheyenne took it and then advanced another cautious step up the stairs. Dust motes drifted in the dry, stale air of the theater. Cheyenne slowly poked her head like a periscope to the level of the stage floor, the light acting like a third eye.

The scream burst from Cheyenne's mouth and Kym instantly imagined the Master's gnarled hands grabbing her by the head and yanking her straight off the stairs and into the darkness.

"What?"

A fat, sleek-furred rat sniffed at the dirty face of a small sleeping child staring at her just inches from the trapdoor's open edge, like it had fallen asleep watching a bug crawl under the hatch's edge. The rat scurried into the darkness as her scream faded away.

"I'm sorry. I got startled."

"No shit. Keep moving for goodness sake."

Cheyenne eased out onto the stage, careful to avoid the children who'd decided to sleep next to the trap door. Kym was right behind her. The stale air was practically

135

mountain fresh compared to the reek of the Master's chamber.

Kim took the flashlight from her and then paused, her breath catching in her chest. Even with the very limited power of the keyring light, she was shocked by the sea of hateful, accusing stares. She recognized the staff and children from the daycare, but the theater was filled with men and women, the elderly, and teenagers representing every race. And they all seemed to be watching Kym and Cheyenne's escape.

"Come on," Cheyenne whispered, sounding a bit stronger.

The two women headed toward the closest set of stairs to the front row of a sold-out theater of vampires.

They stepped over a couple of slumbering members of the Master's army before reaching the heavy curtain separating the short hallway between the theater and the large concession stand. Kym gently pulled the velvety burgundy curtain to the side, almost expecting someone to be standing there. At the far end of the long lobby, the glow of streetlights peeked around the edges of the newspaper plastered on the glass entrance doors on each side of the box office.

"See the light? We're almost there," Kym said, relief in her voice. She wrapped her arm around Cheyenne's waist.

Cheyenne saw the light but instinctively knew her real escape was much more complicated. Simply escaping the Master's lair was hardly reason to celebrate.

The women made their way to the entrance doors, kicking up dust from the filthy carpeted floor. Once they got close, Kym put a finger to her lips and then crept alone up to one of the entrance door's exposed edge of glass. She squinted at the outside world. The streetlights blazed bright amid the nighttime backdrop. The blaring silence of the abandoned theater continued outside to the future revitalized area. Kym peeked to the left and saw the private security car parked in front. It was one of those tiny Smart cars. She ducked back, afraid the rent-a-cop might see her. The small security patrol vehicle was there the evening Timothy loaded them onto a city bus and brought them here. She figured the watchman was under the Master's control.

She tested the door. It seemed unlocked. She glanced back at Cheyenne. She seemed a little better but not up to making a run for it. They were going to need the patrol car.

"I'm going to distract the security guy. When I do, make a run for the patrol car and we'll head straight to the Pacific Grove police station, okay?

Cheyenne nodded, running her hand through her hair. "Okay."

"Here goes nothing," Kym said and then pushed her way out the door, stumbling to the ornate pavement. She started yelling and waving her arms in the chilly air. A second later, the gray-uniformed security officer popped out of the tiny car and the chubby Hispanic man hustled to her side. It was a minor miracle his law enforcement cap didn't fall off.

"Oh my God, oh my God, oh my God," she repeated, getting to her feet and looking around for help.

"What's wrong? What's happening?" the patrolman asked, frantically looking between her and the theater entrance. Kym noticed the car was running. She grabbed the front of the man's uniform and felt the bulletproof vest underneath.

"It's so horrible. Oh my God."

"Is it the Master?"

Kym nodded vigorously. "Yes, yes," she responded and then grabbed the mace from his utility belt and sprayed him in the eyes. The security officer grabbed at his face and screamed like he'd been shot in the balls. He dropped to the sidewalk, and a split-second later Cheyenne burst out of the theater, stumbling toward the patrol car.

Kym laughed at the success of her improvisation and threw the small bottle of mace at the guard, who was rolling back and forth in agony. Kym turned toward the car when the man grabbed her ankle. She jerked her leg away but lost her balance and fell to the pavement. Cheyenne jerked at the passenger door, but it was locked. The security officer snarled and grabbed her ankles again. A menacing wail came from inside the theater. The women's blood ran cold. Kym kicked to free herself, crying out..

"Get out of here! Now!"

Cheyenne froze for a moment and then moved around the car to the open driver's door. She dropped behind the wheel and slammed the door. She watched as the man had crawled up Kym's legs, trying to pin her to the ground. She continued to struggle to free herself as she crawled toward the passenger door. Cheyenne reached across the tiny interior, unlocking the door and pushing it open. The wail swept into the car like a police siren. She didn't know what it meant, but it couldn't be anything good. And then it felt like a feral cat started scratching at her brain. She grabbed her head, the pain so intense she could barely hear Kym's desperate pleas for her to leave her despite her being less than ten feet from the open car door.

And then three things happened simultaneously.

Cheyenne heard Kym's commanding scream to get out, and she grabbed the steering wheel and slammed her foot on the gas pedal.

Kym kicked free of the security guard and got to her feet, grabbing at but missing the open door of the leaving patrol car. She ran into the deserted street and started after the vehicle.

The theater doors flew open, and wailing vampires flowed out like angry wasps from a battered nest. Ignoring the watchman, they filled the street as they chased Kym and the fleeing patrol car.

Cheyenne glanced at the rearview mirror, shocked at the scene behind her. It took her an instant to recognize Kym ahead of the pack of chasing vampires. As much as she wanted to slam on the brakes to give the woman a chance, the fastest of the pursuing mob dragged her down, her screams following the car down the block. Several of the things covered the woman while the others sprinted by and continued their pursuit.

The little car didn't have much acceleration, but it was keeping her out in front. A few blocks down from the theater, a collection of construction signs and barrels marked the future on and off ramps from the neighboring freeway. The lights of Pacific Grove were ahead, and a quick glance behind her showed her pursuers gaining with every block. Without time to weigh the consequences, Cheyenne swerved the car and crashed through the flashing sawhorse barricade and on to the onramp. The car accelerated up the incline, the engine whirring with strain. Seconds later, the dark images of the vampires followed like sharks. The wailing had stopped, but their eerie silence might have been worse.

Suddenly she realized she was driving without headlights. She grabbed at where she thought the knob might be and the lights flashed on just in time to show her what looked like the end of a possibly incomplete ramp.

139

Barrels and flashing lights surrounded her, but it was too late to stop. She tried to aim the car between the two middle barrels. An instant before impact she realized it was going to be too tight—

The wrenching sound of a car's exterior during a collision is the automotive version of a screaming infant. Cheyenne held the steering wheel in a straight-armed death grip, screaming as the econo-box forced its way through, tearing up both sides of the car. She realized the pavement was still under the wheels, so she turned the car to the right. An instant later car horns were blaring around her as headlights filled the car's interior. She jerked the steering to the left, realizing she was on the fucking freeway. Shit. And as crazy as it seemed, the vampires followed.

She floored the gas pedal and veered across the multiple lanes. Her pursuers attempted to follow, but the light late-night traffic wasn't light enough. Blaring horns and screeching tires filled the air as the vampires discovered they couldn't outrun freeway speeds. Cheyenne couldn't tell if there was a series of accidents or a single, terrible, chain-reaction one. She heard cars and trucks hitting each other and the concrete center divider. More than one vehicle went airborne in her rearview mirror.

As she continued down the freeway, no dark figures followed. She kept the small car in the far left commuter lane for a few more miles and then began to look for a familiar exit. She wiped at her face and eyes, unaware she'd started crying at some point.

Once off the freeway, she pulled into a gas station. Steam was escaping from under the bashed-up front end as she coasted into a space by the well-lit bathrooms. She parked but didn't turn off the noisy, laboring engine.

The clawing in her head stopped, replaced by a quiet, amused chuckle. She knew it was Timothy before his voice filled her head.

"You have yourself a good rest of the night. I'll see you soon."

Cheyenne let out a deep breath and wiped her running nose with the back of her hand. She sat, trying to let her head clear. Timothy was right back in it.

"By the way, your friend Kym has become quite the dinner guest. I might even become a fan of sushi."

It took a moment for his words to seep into her mind. Her stomach heaved and she wretched, a string of saliva dangling from her bottom lip. Her head slumped against the middle of the steering wheel, and she jolted in surprise when the car horn didn't sound off.

Cheyenne was bone tired, reeked of nastiness, and needed to take a serious pee, and the one guy who might be able to help was miles and miles away playing middle-class family man. She was so fucked, and as far as she could tell, so was the South Bay, at the very least.

Cheyenne got out of the car, her grubby T-shirt barely reaching her upper thighs. She walked to the women's restroom and tried the metal doorknob. Locked.

From inside, a female voice called out. "I'll be out in a minute."

Cheyenne started to laugh. Did she really have a minute? An hour? Another day to live? Did it really matter? Was she really still alive right now?

Her laughter turned into sobs, and she let herself slide down the gas station wall. When her butt finally found the pavement, she hugged her knees to her chest. She didn't want to die, but she didn't want to become Timothy's whore for eternity. She certainly didn't want to be a toy for the Master, either.

141

Wait. There was one more. She shook her head like something was loose. Suicide was never the answer, no matter how bleak and hopeless the world looked.

Then again, her world had never looked this dark and broken. She'd almost forgotten what a beautiful sunny day looked like.

The Waves weren't going to be able to stand up to these things, and many more innocent people were going to die horrible deaths like Kym and Stallion.

Cheyenne gripped her knees as tight as she could, but the world remained the same. She was alone with no hope. And she was suddenly glad her parents were already dead.

The bathroom door banged open, and she caught it with her dirty foot as the woman walked past. Her sister, Janice, popped into her head. She had to save her. She was all she had left.

She moved to the lone stall and squatted over the broken toilet seat.

So much for suicide. And who was she fooling? She'd never take her own life. She'd have the devil's baby every day before killing herself. If there was a single piece of advice her mother had drilled into her and she'd chosen to believe in, it was with life, there was hope. Suicide was never the answer.

Unless it kept her sister alive and safe.

16

POSTMORTEM

At some point in the evening, Breeze wished Bam would have arrived. The big man would have used his sheer size to push through the ring of police officers to get to him. His big head would fill Breeze's blurry vision. Tears would run from his large, dark eyes. Breeze would be swallowed up in his friend's massive arms, and neither would speak as the first television reporting crew arrived. Death was spreading like a flu bug throughout the Southland, with many more cases on the horizon.

But Bam never showed up. Breeze never called him. Every second his mind spent marinating in the arctic poison of loss and revenge, the less he thought about the Waves. If things got as ugly as he anticipated, he didn't want to risk any of his brothers' lives.

Breeze continued to stare through the cracks in the front walk to his house, as officers managed to keep the media flies from landing on him. Time dissolved and blew away in the tornado of shock, grief, and anger. He didn't know how long he sat on his small front porch. Garbled conversations and movement surrounded him, a police procedural ocean. He was aware of crime scene techs coming and going, stepping around him with courteous respect. Suit wearing detectives spoke to each other and on their cell phones, occasionally looking in his direction with empty expressions. Breeze wept off and on throughout the evening.

The overcast skies eventually cleared and a million stars invaded. The local television vans packed up and leaked away, chasing the next big story. Patrol units began to disburse to their regular beats. Someone came over and squatted behind him, squeezing a shoulder. Breeze didn't respond. The detectives spoke to neighboring homeowners for a few minutes before they wrapped things up. They hadn't spoken to him for a long time.

A detective took the place of the babysitting patrolman, sitting next to him until the crime scene techs completed their duties. He was a bearded Hispanic man, tall with a big belly. His breath mint was at war with his aftershave. Breeze's eyes blazed, continuing to whisper to himself. "She told me an old high school classmate of mine had stopped by earlier." The detective seemed content to simply listen. At some point the detective handed him a business card with his personal cell scribbled on the back, and the remaining police presence left the scene.

He regurgitated cop-speak into the side of Breeze's face, telling him nothing of interest or assistance until-

"We recovered your wife's cell phone. It was submerged in the tub with her body. It appears her killer left it for us to find. There was a video on it-" Before Breeze could speak, the detective shook his head. "We've booked it into evidence. I have to tell you, the suspect clearly shows himself on purpose, and then recorded your family's murder. It's extremely graphic; nothing I'd recommend you watch even if I could share it with you."

One detective recommended he not stay in the house until the crime scene was professionally taken care of. They asked if he had somewhere to go for the night, or if he needed a ride. Breeze muttered he was fine. He heard the detective's voice continue. "It's going to be ruled a double homicide if the preliminary forensics hold up."

Not long after that they were on their way.

When he was alone on the stoop, fresh tears streaked his face.

The evening's shadows surrounded him, becoming a comforting eraser to his world. Breeze pushed up to his feet and headed into the house. Someone had taken care of the breaker because every light was on. Breeze paused just inside, trying to organize his thoughts. He hadn't felt such overwhelming emotions since the night he'd challenged the Piranhas' three best fighters for control over the South Bay.

He could have sent Ant or Jester or even Bam to represent the club in that challenge, but Breeze made a point to everyone that night—the Piranha, the other gangs, even his fellow Waves. That night he became *the* motherfucker of all motherfuckers. He showed everyone who thought he was just the leader of the toughest crew that he was the leader for a reason. After that night, peace came to the dark South Bay streets and alleys because Breeze ordered it from the Pacific Grove emergency room, and the other gangs fell in line. It was why Moon developed feelings for him, and just about every girl over the age of thirteen would have dropped their panties for him in a street race second.

Doleman had come all the way from the South Bay to get to Breeze's family. How had he known where he and his wife even lived? A second later, the answer popped into his head.

Cheyenne.

Cheyenne had known. She'd sent a wedding card to Breeze and his bride. Bam had given her the fucking address.

She knew a lot. She'd been around at the beginning when a handful of them hung out at the Grove's downtown park wearing aqua and black T-shirts. They didn't even have a name yet. They were just some friends hanging out and watching each other's backs. Most of them couldn't even drive yet.

Breeze turned out lights as he moved from room to room. He avoided the master bathroom. The light could just stay on until he returned. If he returned.

Eventually, Breeze stepped back out the front door, dressed in jeans, a black T-shirt, and tennis shoes, carrying a military-style duffle bag and a small backpack. He turned off the entryway light and locked the front door. He tossed his bags toward the garage door as he moved to the minivan. The garage door started up with a quiet rattle, the light illuminating the space. Parked inside to the right was a covered car. He jerked the dusty car cover off, letting it billow to the concrete floor.

The 1969 Mach 1 Mustang sat at the ready. The custom black and bronze paint job glistened fresh from its last detail.

Breeze hadn't taken the Beast for a real drive since his wedding day. He'd driven it to the church, but had left it for Gypsy to use and then park back at their new valley home. Gypsy had been all excited to finally drive the Beast, but after the reception he had a couple of drinks and decided not to tempt fate. The church pastor allowed him to park it in the garage until he picked it back up the next day. And even then he'd skipped the joyriding and drove it straight to Breeze's and garaged it, safe and sound.

146

Breeze slipped behind the wheel. The engine turned over with a hushed growl, and the car rolled clear of its spot. Breeze slipped the car into park, used the opener to close the garage door, and then popped the trunk release. He tossed his bags in and closed the lid before backing down the driveway.

The Mustang roared down the street. Timothy Doleman wanted him, and now he was going to get him. Every inch and every ounce.

Breeze turned on the radio. An advertisement was just ending. The voice of Marvin Gaye filled the Mustang. The Wave leader couldn't help but sniffle and whimper along to the anthem "Trouble Man.

Breeze's thoughts were like buckshot blasting out of a sawed-off shotgun. The drive back to the South Bay felt like a series of polaroid snapshots. He reluctantly called his mother-in-law and listened as she cried and wailed over her loss. He promised he would get revenge, but she didn't seem to understand. It was going to be a difficult and confusing time for people without full knowledge of the situation. He decided not to reach out to his family until it was all over.

Late-evening weekend traffic on the 405 freeway eased as the Mustang passed the major westside exits for UCLA and Santa Monica and the 10 freeway west to the water. The traffic flow eased even more as folks headed to LAX airport, one of the busiest in the country.

As the city blurred by, Breeze's mind skipped through memories of his abbreviated marriage. Hell, it was more an extended honeymoon. He'd been so happy with his new life and bright future he was almost eager to walk away from The Waves and really start his new life. Now there

147

was nothing but a point blank shotgun blast hole where his heart and guts used to be.

The problem was there weren't nearly enough great memories of Judi and none of his unborn child. Timothy had stolen that from him.

He kept thinking about putting his hand on Judi's pregnant basketball belly that morning. He'd kissed her on the lips, then bent down and kissed their baby goodbye. She'd told him she loved him, but he couldn't remember if he said it back. He told her that he loved her all the time, but had he that last time? The more he thought about it, the less sure he became.

Breeze's focus on the road sharpened as his reminiscing waned. The South Bay exit he wanted was only a couple miles away. He glanced at the speedometer. The Beast was eating up the road at eighty-five. He'd been fortunate not to have been pulled over. His vision blurred as a fresh set of tears threatened to spill down his face, but this time around fewer fell.

When Breeze reached the All Night Garage, the self-service section appeared closed. The streetlight on the corner was out again. Saturday and Sunday evenings tended to be slow. Do-it-yourself mechanics tended to call it quits by dinner time to spend the evenings with their families. Tonight was no exception.

Breeze went straight inside the small apartment off the business office he used to stay in after high school graduation. It had been a great deal—he'd agreed to work full time at the garage, and his father had agreed he could move out of the house and into the cozy quarters at the shop. It was so funny—on the streets, Wallace "Breeze" Thornton was not only considered a grown man but the unofficial president of the South Bay's gang hierarchy, yet

to his parents, recent high school gradu
was still striving for independence and adu

17

.KED THE CHILDREN?

The theme song from the classic sitcom *Gilligan's Island* caused Sailor to jolt awake and fumble for his cell phone. It had been a long night patrolling Pacific Grove. It'd felt good to be back out in public wearing the official Wave colors, though he and the other Waves concentrated on the back alleys surrounding the main drags and the Walk, Pacific Grove's outdoor retail, dining, and entertainment area.

Crater had split them into groups of three. Sailor had spent the night with Ant and Whisper. It had been an interesting night, but no vampire action. He'd gotten home about an hour after dawn and flopped on his bed, barely kicking his tennis shoes off before falling asleep.

Fumbling for his phone, he had no idea what time it was. "Hello?"

"Is this Minnow Tours?" It was a woman's voice. She sounded on the younger side.

Sailor cleared his voice. "Yes it is. How can I help you?"

"Well, I know this is a bit last minute, but are you available for a quick tour of the Pacific Grove shoreline at sunset this evening?"

Sailor's mind ran through the upcoming schedule. He didn't have anything until midweek but quickly double checked the calendar on his phone. He'd remembered correctly. He'd be able to make a little extra cash before heading back to Pacific Grove tonight. It was already early afternoon.

"Well, you're in luck. The boat is available for a couple of hours around that time. How many passengers?"

"Just one," she said and then paused. "Well, two really. It's a little weird." When Sailor didn't ask, she continued. "I've got my grandfather's ashes. He used to spend a lot of time at the Pacific Grove beach when he was young. I just thought it would be a great place to spread his ashes."

"You know that's against the law, right?" Sailor smiled in the dead air. "I'm just kidding. You wouldn't be the first or the last to charter a burial at sea. Let's work through the details, all right?"

"Thank you. I'll see you tonight at eight," she answered politely, sounding a bit relieved.

———————

Tangerine hung up and looked at Timothy and the Master. She smiled enough to show her fangs.

"It's almost too easy," Timothy said.

The Master smiled, the corruption behind it causing Tangerine and Timothy to take a step back. "Wars aren't won on the battlefield. They're won in conference rooms where strategy is formulated and attacks and counter attacks are planned. Don't you two ever play Xbox?"

When the Master laughed, Timothy and Tangerine flinched at the high-pitched, nasally whine.

151

"Tonight is going to be the next big step toward our domination. Don't fail me." His focus shifted from them to the shadowy floor across the room. He beckoned with a single deadly talon.

"Please me," he commanded.

Out of the shadows crawled a naked Kym. Sections of her body appeared raw where large areas of skin had been peeled away. She crawled and cringed like an abused pet. The Master leaned back in his lounger throne and closed his eyes. Kym's moist eyes darted up to Tangerine and Timothy. Tangerine simply grinned back at her, while Timothy looked away.

"Make it good, or I'll have more of your skin for a snack, bitch."

The woman mumbled something that sounded like, "Yes, Master, I understand," but Timothy wasn't sure. Kym's escape attempt complicated things for the moment, but Timothy was confident in his ability to control Cheyenne; he just didn't want to fully do that. He wanted her to willingly give herself to him, and proudly stand by his side. That was something he wasn't as confident in. And the more he thought about it, the more he realized Breeze wasn't the real problem. It was him, and he didn't know exactly how to overcome that obstacle.

Timothy turned and walked away before Kym's head lowered over the Master's lap. The obscene sounds of her mouth on him might as well have been the screams of infants burning in a hospital fire. Timothy exhaled softly, fighting to ignore his fading emotions and withering morality. He tried to tell himself that if she hadn't tried to escape, she wouldn't have been tortured, but the reasoning was hollow at best. The Master was a soulless creature—a spider in human form. A demon who offered shiny, golden trinkets splattered with blood and loved to mimic the screams of the innocent.

Timothy just cared about having Cheyenne. The rest could burn to ash and he wouldn't give it a second thought. But this chosen stroll through Hell wasn't as easy to ignore as he'd tried to tell himself.

Timothy started up the ladder to the theater stage. If she made one, Kym's next escape attempt would be suicide.

Midafternoon on that Sunday, Zero sat on the curb in downtown Los Angeles gnawing on a fresh carrot. His phone hadn't rung in an hour, which wasn't unusual. He felt a little strung out after the all-nighter the Waves had pulled. He'd covered the pier and beach with Surgeon and Whisper. The night had been quiet and uneventful, but he felt like he needed a couple more hours of sleep. He'd found himself wishing Breeze had been involved but totally understood his true leader's situation. Nothing was more important than honor to one's family. He took a sip from a plastic water bottle and then finished the last couple of swallows. He looked around the tall buildings surrounding him. The Los Angeles downtown skyline was hardly worth mentioning compared to Manhattan's. Now that was a metropolitan business center.

His phone buzzed instead of rang. It felt less intrusive to him. Zero fished it out of his pocket. It was work. He put it on speaker.

"Courier one, we have a pickup in your old stomping grounds. You want it?"

"Sure. Details please." He activated his phone's recorder.

"The dispatcher was all business. "Pacific Grove. The Bastion Theater. Seven o'clock. Small package."

Zero frowned. "Are you sure? The Bastion's been closed for years."

"I took the call myself. The package is going to the All Night Garage on Lewis. Extra rush. Double fee."

The Wave's hangout? It couldn't be a coincidence.

"I got it. Thank you." He ended the call and immediately called Surgeon and then Whisper. They would meet him at the theater at 6:45. Maybe they'd get a break in this crazy Scooby Doo mystery they were involved in.

———⚬———

Longstreet took an extra lap around the park's walking path with his German shepherd, Axel. He couldn't be sure, but his instincts were blaring that he was being followed. It was odd being blind—he'd quickly learned to feel and deflect the extra attention being without sight afforded him. Eyes were always on him, acknowledging his sensory disadvantage. Some people merely observed his uniqueness while others became mesmerized by their pity. Axel hadn't alerted him to anything potentially threatening, but he could sense, almost feel someone's attention focused on him for an extended amount of time. Like a prolonged stare, it brushed against the skin on the back of his neck, gently resting there like a feather.

The extra time in the park had to be putting it close to sundown. He still needed to get home, get cleaned up and dressed for another night on one of Pacific Grove's mainline buses. He'd drawn the duty from Crater. Ride the different buses and keep his ears open. People talked about things on public transportation. Rumors, news reports, weird shit. It was the weird shit the Waves were interested in, and Longstreet happily accepted the assignment. He was more than capable of handling himself in a one-on-one altercation, but chaotic melees put him at an extreme disadvantage. This duty was perfect for him, and he already knew a couple of the night shift drivers, so cruising for an extended amount of time wasn't a problem.

The problem was, who the hell was following him around?

"Bench," he said softly to Axel, and the dog guided him to his right and then slowed and straightened his course. Longstreet dropped his hand and ran his fingers along the wooden bench seat. He estimated the middle and sat, feeling Axel drop and relax along his foot. Axel wouldn't allow anyone to sit down next to him without a quiet warning growl. He could hear the dog's quiet pant, and he imagined his guide's head staying on a subtle swivel. Longstreet focused outside his own heartbeat and listened to the passing walkers and joggers and bike riders. The early evening traffic was much less than it had been when they'd first started out. The sensory stew around him was smells and sounds. People spoke on their phones, some holding conversations best left in private. The wafting scent of a soiled diaper wrinkled his nose, as did the passing fragrance of soap and perspiration. The heavy, plodding steps of a first-time jogger lumbered past and then a pair of speed-walking seniors cruised by. He anticipated their hellos a split second before they uttered them, and he politely returned their greeting. There was a quiet pause to the traffic and then came footsteps that caught his attention. Whoever was approaching caught Axel's attention too. Longstreet felt the dog's body become more rigid. Then came the whisper-quiet growl.

155

A pair of walkers. Both sets of footsteps were light to the ground, and both slowed just a bit as they were passing the bench. Longstreet imagined a young child and perhaps its grandparent, which didn't make much sense explaining Axel's reaction.

"Good evening," he forced out with a pleasant smile.

There wasn't a response, though the child growled back at Axel. He was hushed, and then an older woman's voice said, "Be nice."

Longstreet felt the intensity of their stares. Intense. Hungry. Hateful.

Axel popped up to a seated position, surprising him. They left a faint hint of sugary candy and dried blood in their wake. Their footsteps faded until they'd moved a safe distance away. Axel's body language remained on alert.

A small child and a senior citizen posing a threat? Longstreet's mind replayed recent events. There'd been news stories involving Papa Midnight's senior community, and the ongoing investigation of the missing preschoolers and staff. Was there a connection between the two? Longstreet sat and mulled the news stories over. Authorities weren't sharing a lot of details about either incident. Other than both taking place in Pacific Grove in the last few days, Longstreet couldn't connect the dots from one to the other. Maybe someone else could. Or maybe the dots would become more aligned.

It was time to get home. Axel sensed it and stood. Seconds later he was tugging Longstreet toward his beach end cottage.

Bam hung up and stared across the nearly empty parking lot of the Sunset Dunes Retirement Community. A patrol car sat at the front entrance, and Bam saw yellow crime scene tape outlining the front entrance. The parking lot was empty because authorities had suggested residents temporarily stay with family or friends until the investigation was over. The Pacific Grove police had stationed a patrol car for the safety of the residents refusing to vacate or those with nowhere else to go.

Bam looked across the cab at Crater. "My contact at the station is going to make a call. We'll get about fifteen minutes to take a look at Papa Midnight's apartment. That's it."

Crater shrugged. "Better than nothing. We'll make it work."

The two Waves looked back across the busy six-lane road, waiting for a sign to move. A minute passed. Then another. The sun continued to drop lower and lower in the sky. Sunset was less than an hour away.

After five long minutes, the two looked at each other. Bam could only shrug his massive shoulders. When his phone rang, it came close to startling them both.

"Hello?" Bam answered. He listened and then frowned at Crater. "All right, we'll go take a look." Bam started up his vehicle. "He can't reach the patrolmen across the radio or their cell phones."

"Maybe—" Crater started and then stopped. The sprawling three-floor senior complex now looked menacing, looming half in and out of end-of-day shadows. The flags at the entrance hung down along their poles, dead without a hint of wind. The sprawling community was snap shot still.

157

"Let's just get in and out, okay?" Bam said, unwilling to start up a conversation revealing he had the same reservations.

Bam drove across the road and into the community parking lot. Thirty-six hours ago the lot had been nearly full, and Papa Midnight was alive and talking and joking and then he was dead. Simple as that.

Bam thought, *Fuck it*, and pulled up at the entrance, across from the Pacific Grove police car. No one was inside. Bam and crater turned and looked through the tall and wide glass doors that led inside the main atrium. The lights were on, but no one, not even the front desk concierge, was home.

The Waves got out of Bam's pickup and walked inside, both men taking sneaky glances at the sun and the horizon on a sure collision course. Bam jogged through the automatic doors with Crater right behind. The full evening lights weren't on yet, so the lobby was growing dark with shadows. All the visitor chairs were empty, and the usual golden oldies background music was nonexistent. Crime scene tape made a loopy circle in front of the information desk. Inside it was the outline of a body. The two Waves paused, thinking about Papa Midnight and how he'd died. Bam looked up and through the main hall, and for a moment it reminded him of the open jaws of a great white shark.

Crater nudged him in the back and then whispered like they were in a library. "Where are the cops?"

"I have no fucking idea," Bam whispered back, walking again but at a slightly slower pace.

The east wing hallway was eerily empty and quiet. No muted conversations or loud television programs. Just quiet. Unnatural quiet. The elevator opened right up, empty and waiting. No music serenaded them to the third floor, where no one was waiting. They turned down the corridor, and Crater couldn't help but glance back down the hallway.

Papa Midnight's apartment door was blocked by more crime scene tape. The Waves paused, and then Bam snatched off the tape and turned the doorknob. He paused for a second.

"What's wrong?"

Bam glanced up and down the empty hallway. "You hear that?"

"Come on," Crater said, pushing into the apartment. "Let's do what we need to and get out of here. The place is like a fucking tomb."

Bam stood a moment longer, listening, and then followed his friend.

It didn't take thirty seconds to locate Papa Midnight's laptop. Bam sat at the dining room table and turned it on while Crater took a look around.

"He sure was neat," Crater observed, hesitant to touch any of the dead man's things out of respect.

Bam stared at the computer screen, frustrated. "I don't have his password. Shit."

"Can't you, I don't know, figure it out?"

"This isn't a fucking movie," Bam growled, slamming the device shut.

Crater threw up his hands. "Sorry."

"I'm not sure why we're here," Bam said, looking around his mentor's place.

Glimpses of the man were everywhere. A picture caught Bam's eye, and he moved from the table to a bookcase in the cozy living room. It was a black and white photo of Bam, his father, and Papa Midnight outside the downtown

159

Los Angeles library. Bam was a little boy, maybe seven or eight. Both men were beaming. At the time, Bam didn't understand the significance of his dad's first day as the library's director, but he certainly understood it fully now. The men were in their prime, their lives ahead of them. Now both men were gone, unable to pass along their great knowledge to Bam's future children. The thought was so profoundly certain Bam's eyes moistened.

"Hey," Crater called out from the other room. "There's some books here that could help."

Bam sniffled and swiped across his eyes. "Coming." He started to put the picture back but changed his mind, cradling it in a huge hand.

As he stepped next to Crater, there was a muted crash. Glass breaking? Then another one.

"You hear that?"

Bam listened to the third muffled crash. It sounded closer.

"The hall?" Crater asked, moving toward the front door. He leaned toward the peephole. The closest hallway light burst in a shower of glass and sparks. The corridor got gloomy.

"I think we ought to get out of here," he whispered.

"Let's go," the big man agreed.

There was another crash further down the hall.

"Fuck. Someone's taking out the lights."

The two Waves looked at each other.

"Are we trapped?" Crater said. The truth crept into the men's guts.

Crater flipped the deadbolt and latched the chain. He shrugged. "Can't hurt."

Bam pulled out his cell phone and tried his police contact. It went straight to voicemail. He left a quick message.

"Screw this," he said and then tapped 911. The emergency line went straight into the automated system. Bam hung up.

He started to call Breeze but stopped.

"Could just be vandals," Crater said.

"If we're lucky," Bam said. "Could be what took care of Papa Midnight."

"Old doesn't mean soft," Crater said. "Ready?"

Bam nodded. "Waves crash."

Crater nodded and opened the door and they stepped out in the hall. It was gloomy without the lighting, but they could see.

"Old doesn't mean soft," Bam whispered, looking at one end of the corridor and then the other.

Three or four elderly folks stood at each end. Their expressions were feral, like rabid animals. They were in various stages of dress and undress. In that regard, both Waves were relieved for the poor lighting. That relief vanished when both groups rushed the two men. When their attackers were halfway to them, Bam and Crater stepped forward to deliver the first blows. In seconds they were swarmed over by the hissing, growling vampires. Their strength and speed were surprising. The Waves could barely hold them off.

"The elevator!" Crater called out, the vampires ripping and clawing at his clothing.

Bam defensively met the attack, but his survival instinct kicked in, and he began to use his strength to the maximum. Adrenalin made the pain of their slicing talons feel distant. He heard Crater's directive as he grabbed the frail but strong as a bull great-grandmother and slammed her into the wall, the back of her small head bursting like a ripe tomato. He used her limp form as a shield, forcing the other two back. He glanced over his shoulder and saw Crater struggling to keep on his feet. They were ripping him to pieces. He didn't have much longer. Bam grabbed one of his attackers by the arm and threw him head over heels into Crater's pack, scattering them.

"Run!" Bam shouted, turning and plowing straight through his remaining old woman like a screen door. He paused just long enough to stomp her face nearly flat into the carpet. It exploded like a rotten pumpkin.

Bam ran toward the elevator end, expecting Crater to be right behind him. The bloodcurdling scream made Bam lumber to a stop. He turned and blinked the blood and sweat from his eyes, thinking he'd just witnessed a magic trick.

Crater was gone. Just like that.

Instead of his buddy in black and aqua running toward him to safety, he was nowhere to be seen.

Then Bam refocused on the savage pile on the floor where Crater was standing. Now there were old people covered with blood, clawing underneath themselves, their pale, wrinkled faces smeared with blood. The sounds that carried down to Bam were the sounds of his friend being eaten alive. It was one hundred times worse than the night with Doleman and Cheyenne. The last gurgling breaths of Henry "Crater" Wilson would haunt Bam for the rest of his life. Bam wanted to go back and smash them all to sacks of broken bones, but he knew Crater was dead.

"Fuck!" Bam cried out, turning the corner and pressing the elevator call button. He'd get Breeze and the others and they'd come back and kill every one of these motherfuckers for Crater and Papa Midnight.

The elevator door slid open, and Bam froze. The animal hisses and snarls reached his ears an instant before his eyes registered the lift crowded with more elderly vampires. Enraged, Bam forced himself into the ravenous pack while the red-eyed, bloodthirsty mob grabbed and clawed the big man inside the elevator, their individual, unnatural strength magnified by their sheer numbers. He punched and elbowed, but for all his great strength, Bam's struggle against his death was useless. As the flesh was torn from his body, Bam realized he'd dropped the photo of him and his dad back in the hallway. With talons and fangs tearing the life from his massive body, Crater's last breaths wouldn't be haunting Bam very much longer.

He stared into the feral eyes of a one hundred-year-old man as one of the things ripped his throat out. Bam's own blood blinded him before the vampire horde took his eyes. He was dead before his mind could register his gruesome demise.

Waves crash.

———✦———

Axel growled deep in his throat, alerting Longstreet something was wrong as he waved his access card over the lock sensor. There was a beep and then a quiet click as the deadbolt disengaged. He started to push the door open and thought he heard a child giggle. Longstreet started inside but realized Axel didn't move. He could imagine the German shepherd staring into the gloom of his place.

"Come on, boy," Longstreet said, tugging at the guide bar. The dog reluctantly obeyed, the soft growl continuing.

The front door swung shut as Longstreet released the dog and then pulled off his black and aqua hoodie. He took another step and immediately bumped into a chair. A small child giggled somewhere off to his right. Axel barked and then growled with menace.

"All right, who's here?"

Another giggle, this time from his left. The hair on the back of his neck stood up. Longstreet took a step back, and for the first time in a long time, he felt the full burden of his blindness.

"Enough already. This isn't funny." As soon as the words left his mouth, he wished he'd said something else. A smattering of giggles surrounded him, and Axel's growl turned into a frightened whine. As his mind whirled, he caught a faint hint of blood.

"Boo!" came a little kid's voice right behind him.

Longstreet jumped, the room suddenly filled with children's laughter, and someone small jumped on his back. The kid's laughter was in his ear. In the next instant, Longstreet screamed as small knives raked across the side of his head, pulling it to the left before something sharp plunged into his exposed throat. He lost his balance and fell, his hands struggling to pull off his attacker.

Axel was barking and growling, his paws scrambling on the hardwood floor. Several others quickly joined the attack, ripping and grabbing all over his body, the notion of dying flashing through his mind. He could hear Axel fighting, and there was a sudden sharp yelp from his companion and then nothing. The sounds filling Longstreet's ears were primal, slobbering feeding sounds. A tear of pain streaked down his face when he realized what he was hearing was coming from the assault on his own body.

164

Down at the marina, Sailor piloted his tour boat along the South Bay coastline, heading north toward the bright lights of the Pacific Grove pier. Even at a distance the rotating, flashing lights of the giant Ferris wheel and the rollercoaster were a beacon to young and young at heart fun seekers. The burnt-orange sun had begun to disappear into the horizon. It was a sight that never got old for the tour guide Wave. Despite its alluring beauty, Sailor noticed his passenger, a pale but pretty young woman named Tangerine, seemed to find him more interesting to look at. She sat in one of the high back fishing chairs, pivoting between the picturesque sunset and the boat's captain. She'd just look at him, her expression odd enough to make Sailor wonder what was on her mind. She was pretty, especially for guys into piercings. She didn't talk much, and he was pretty sure her hands had never left the decorative box she'd brought on board.

"Just a few more minutes," he called to her. She smiled just a little and then reluctantly turned back to the sunset. Sailor looked at the back of her chair. He wasn't sure how old she was—maybe late teens? He was set to turn twenty-three in a month.

"Don't look for trouble where there is none," Sailor whispered to himself. He'd heard Breeze say that phrase a gazillion times over the years. Something he'd gotten from his father. Just solid common sense. And this was no time for romance. Focus.

The pier was coming up. Sailor throttled the engine down and turned away from the wheel to speak to her, but she'd already turned back toward him. Instead of feeling flattered, something in his gut signaled caution.

165

"Uh, is this a good spot?"

Tangerine stood up and set the box on the seat. She seemed to float to him, stopping just a little closer than she needed to.

"What do you think?" It wasn't so much a question as it seemed like just something to say.

Sailor cleared his throat, resisting the screaming urge to step back. "I think it's a good spot. Sure."

"Okay," the young woman answered.

Then came an awkward moment. Sailor expected her to turn and move to get the box, but she didn't. She didn't move a muscle. And in that moment, it struck Sailor that Tangerine hadn't taken her sunglasses off. Her long fashion nails took on an ominous look.

"Uh, are you going to need any help?"

The young woman tilted her head. She seemed to be studying him. "No. I can take care of it all by myself." She finally turned and drifted back to the fishing chair.

He finally exhaled.

He watched her pick up the box and wander to the boat's stern. She looked to her left, watching the sun disappear. With the engine off, the sound of the ocean surrounded them. Sailor watched Tangerine stand and stare out over the ocean. He wasn't sure if she was watching the sunset disappear, the ocean itself, or was mulling over memories of her grandfather. Somehow, the longer she stood, the more unnatural her stillness seemed.

Tangerine thawed as the sun disappeared. She opened the box, but instead of tipping it over the side, she set it back down on the fishing chair. She turned and looked at him, finally sliding off the sunglasses and setting them next to the box.

As she started toward him, Sailor wondered what color her eyes were. She passed through the shadows, and when she stepped into the cabin's light, Sailor's mouth dropped open. He wasn't sure which was worse—her blood-red eyes or her predator smile. The next thing he knew he was on the deck staring up into her face, her expression wild. She plunged her hands into his chest, and he screamed, as much by the impossible act as the paralyzing pain. The ocean swallowed the sound of his agony, and Tangerine used the box for what it was intended.

The fiery setting sun cast long, deep shadows in Pacific Grove when Zero came to a smooth stop behind Surgeon's black Supra in front of the old Bastion Theater. Zero leaned the racing motorcycle on its kickstand and then stepped off, setting his helmet on the small passenger roost. Parked a couple of blocks down the street, a private security car suddenly took off, turning out of sight at the next intersection. *Probably vandals or homeless folks,* Zero thought before he peeked into Surgeon's sweet ride. Whisper's custom skateboard was propped on the passenger seat. Zero glanced at his phone. It was six forty-eight. He was hardly late. A quiet rattle pulled his attention toward one of the lobby double doors. He unzipped his custom black and aqua leather riding jacket and moved toward the doors. He grabbed a metal handle and was surprised when it pulled open. The lobby was musky and the lack of light swallowed up the concession stand at the far end of the long lobby. It offered a murky invitation he easily refused.

Zero stepped back outside and tapped out a quick text to his Wave brothers. He wandered back to his bike, awaiting a reply.

None came.

It was a couple minutes before seven. The street was abandoned. A gust of wind carried part of a newspaper across the street.

"Where are you guys?" Zero whispered.

The front of the abandoned theater stared back at him. It was as dead as the rest of the neighborhood. He couldn't remember the last movie he'd seen there. They'd built the crazy Galaxy 20 down by the pier with the stadium seating and the great sound systems. It was game over for everyone else once it opened.

Zero checked his phone. It was seven o'clock. He wanted to go in as much as he liked picking up his girlfriend's tarantula. He grabbed a small flashlight out of his kit and returned to the door. As he opened it, one of the heavy velvety curtains that led into the theater pulled back just a bit.

"You the courier?" a man's voice asked from the other side. It didn't belong to either of his friends. Zero followed the flashlight's strong beam.

"Yeah, that's me."

The heavy drape opened more as he approached. He stepped into the theater and the curtain dropped behind him.

———————

Outside, the security patrol car and a large flatbed tow truck pulled up, the tow truck pulling in front of the black Supra and then backing up to get in position to tow the sports car. Once it was secured, he maneuvered to take the racing bike too. When the motorcycle was ready to transport, the tow truck drove off and the security patrol car pulled in front of the long-closed Bastion Theater. No one came back out.

An entry door eventually pushed open, and a lumpy duffel bag was tossed out onto the sidewalk. The security guard casually exited his car, approached the entrance, locked the doors, picked up the canvas bag, and took it with him back to the car's trunk. He drove away, his mission a simple delivery.

18

THE LAST BOY SCOUT

The muscles in Breeze's arms flexed and bulged as he continued his series of push-ups. The exertion of the simple exercise helped distract his mind from the slobbering mental maw of madness threatening to swallow him every second. The office TV droned on as his T-shirt dampened with sweat. When his shaking arms couldn't complete another, he collapsed on the polished concrete floor. Heart pounding in his ears, the droning words of the late-night replay of the evening news broadcast became less and less jumbled. The disinterested flirting of the information at the edge of his mind slowly became a direct reporting of the world of Pacific Grove.

He wasn't looking at the TV screen as the female reporter's voice fought a losing battle with her fear. "I'm at the intersection of Pacific Grove Boulevard and Uno Avenue—"

A series of blaring emergency sirens flew by, drowning her out. Breeze couldn't tell what combination of police, fire truck, or ambulance roared by.

"Pacific Grove is in the midst of a frenzy of violent crime like nothing in South Bay history. Communities bordering Pacific Grove have also seen emergency service calls skyrocket during the last forty-eight hours. Record numbers of absent first responders aren't helping

170

matters, and Pacific Grove's emergency dispatch has been overwhelmed—"

The sound of a helicopter flying over the news crew broke into the reporter's monologue.

"Channel 6 News has reached out to both the Pacific Grove's mayor's office and chief of police, but there's been no response. In the meantime, prominent community leaders have advised all South Bay citizens to stay at home, locking all doors and windows. It's also been advised to not answer your doors after sunset due to a staggering amount of reports of unmotivated assaults by strangers. Right now, Pacific Grove and its neighboring communities have become a dangerous warzone. This is Sandra Zalman, Channel 6—"

Breeze looked up in time to see several people run through her shot, nearly knocking her off her feet. They were yelling and screaming, and more than one warned the news crew to run. By the time the reporter got her bearings, the camerawoman had broken her professional training and the live camera shot turned back in the direction the fleeing people had come from. The camera barely held still long enough for the viewing audience to see the approaching danger. The momentary camera shot was of the shadowy darkness of Uno a block or so south of Pacific Grove. The images of dark figures moving toward the news crew was undeniable. The camerawoman barked some Spanish profanity and the camera dropped to the ground, the angle still pointing toward the approaching mob. The anchorwoman yelped off camera, followed by the sound of fleeing footsteps, doors slamming, and the sound of a vehicle screeching off. The station cut off the camera feed before the pursuing figures burst clear of the shadows.

One odd detail struck Breeze. There'd been no sound from the mob. No threats or shrieks or shouts. The clip had been so brief, there hadn't been time to pick up anything else. Were vampires really taking over Pacific Grove?

Breeze's head pounded. He hadn't eaten since the snack he'd had at the beach outing. Dinner got waylaid by the unexpected nightmare in the valley. He needed to keep his strength up. He took out his cell phone as he hung the metal chin up bar across the door frame.

The automated response for Mama Italy's came on after a couple of rings. The South Bay's popular pizza joint stayed busy from open to close. The recording asked the customer to hold the line. It wasn't the first time an elevator version of the Lionel Richie song "All Night Long" had serenaded him. When it finished, a Beach Boys hit followed. It was just about over when it sounded like someone picked up. All kinds of loud commotion came from the restaurant's end.

"Hello?" Breeze said. It sounded like the handset jostled and then bounced off the counter and the floor. Then a woman's scream knifed through his cell phone's speaker. There was an awkward gurgle and what sounded like the cackle of a fairy-tale witch. Then the line went dead.

"Hello? Hello?" Breeze listened for a moment but no reply. He stared at his phone like it was a dead bug. It took several seconds for the horrible truth to seep into his mind. He tossed his phone on the bedside table and slowly sank to the bed. The horror was spreading like an infectious plague.

He was at a disadvantage. Doleman seemed to know much more about him than he did about the deli owner. He didn't have a lot of time to do research. He needed to get on the offensive, strike back fast and hard. He needed to even the playing field.

But how could he when he was outmatched and outnumbered?

Calling Bam and Crater was a constant urge, but he needed a way to get his revenge while putting his guys in the least amount of danger. This was no street fight with a rival gang. It was the middle of the night now, but it wasn't going to be long before local news stations would be carrying the story of his tragedy, and the guys would be blowing up his phone. At the moment that was the least of his problems.

Breeze moved to the chin-up bar. It wasn't long before a dew of sweat joined the moisture in his eyes. Grief and anger and fear began to give way to numbness and exhaustion.

From what he knew about vampires, real or fiction, there was usually a master, like Dracula, holed up somewhere pulling all the strings. Timothy couldn't be at the top of the food chain. Someone, or something, had made him. Which meant Breeze had two enemies to dispose of. Shit.

Breeze couldn't remember ever having a squawk with Doleman. Especially something big enough to have led to the slaughtering of his family. Whatever it was, Doleman shouldn't have made it personal. He shouldn't have involved his family.

Now, simply killing him wouldn't be enough.

It would never be enough.

Doing chin-ups until exhaustion, he grabbed a towel from the small bathroom and swiped his face. He drifted to the office's front window and peeked through the blinds. It was dark and quiet outside. No distant sirens. Breeze was about to let the blinds close when something moved by the front gate. Without the illumination from the corner streetlight, the shadows were deep by the street, but it was definitely a person. For a moment it appeared to be a big dog lying on the sidewalk at his feet. Longstreet's guide dog, Axel, came to mind. The dark shape was about the size of the big German shepherd, but without the small, telling details. And whatever it was, it wasn't moving. No wagging tail, no flinching ears. As Breeze was able to focus, the more it appeared to be a large duffel bag. He released the blind. Curious. Someone dropping off something this late? Auto parts maybe. Maybe a homeless person confused in the darkness about the location. He needed to take a closer look.

Breeze was already moving toward the garage's office entrance, grabbing the gate opener off the wall key hooks. He stepped outside, a wisp of wind tickling his perspiring skin as he followed the driveway up to the gate. Halfway there he pressed the opener, the wrought iron gate swinging smooth and silent. Breeze stopped walking and suddenly he pressed it again. The man didn't move as the gate swing closed. Breeze's heart began to pound in his chest. He was just close enough to recognize the shadowy figure.

"Lobo," Breeze said. The leader of the Piranhas slowly thawed. He reached down and tossed what he'd brought with him easily over the wrought iron gate.

Zipped end to end, the black military duffle appeared lumpy. Suddenly Breeze wished he had grabbed the mag-light when he'd grabbed the opener. He took another step forward. Lobo stood unnaturally still. His face was hidden by the deep shadows.

"What are you doing here?"

"I volunteered to deliver this gift," Lobo said. "I've been thinking about ripping your throat out since I was … changed."

Breeze stiffened. He'd stepped out into the night unarmed, oblivious to the potential danger. Lobo could scale the iron gate and kill him if he wanted. Something was holding him back.

"The Master says you belong to Timothy, so I can't touch you. A part of me hopes you find a way to defeat Timothy so I can find you, one night soon, in the darkness."

Before Breeze could think of how to respond, Lobo turned and sprinted away. The Wave leader instinctively moved to the gate for a better look.

The street was empty. Empty and graveyard quiet.

He looked at the duffel and then picked it up by the handles. It was substantial but not heavy, and the contents seemed to jostle. He headed back inside, dread tickling his gut.

Breeze stepped into the office, setting the bag on top of the main desk. An odd, faint smell wafted from it. The Wave leader jerked the large zippers apart to reveal the contents.

Inside was Bam's large severed head, his empty eye sockets staring through Breeze and into eternity. Breeze cried out and fell back into the other desk. Shock froze him.

It wasn't the only one in the bag. The fucking duffel was full of heads.

A scream filled Breeze's ears, and it took him a moment to realize the scream was his. In an act of desperation, Breeze lunged at the duffel and attempted to close it. The zipper closed past Bam's face but got stuck. He jerked at it, but the zipper stayed open long enough for him to see Zero's face peering out, his eyes lifeless and dull. He stumbled away from the bag, frantically wiping his hands on his jeans as if he could wipe away the horror of their deaths.

"Fuck!" he roared, his mind spinning to the edge of oblivion. He clutched at the door frame, steading himself. Breeze stared at the bag, his eyes wide in disbelief.

How many heads were in the bag? Whose heads? Only one way to find out, but Breeze trembled.

"No," he said to himself, realizing the solution but rejecting it. "Never again."

The Wave leader turned away and reentered the apartment, slamming the door. His chest began to hitch. He dropped to the bed sobbing. The losses were more than he could carry. The night had finished him.

Tobey Freeman walked up to the enclosed bus stop and dropped down on the vacant mental bench. He gave himself a quick look-over. His Boy Scout uniform looked good enough to hang back in his closet. His shirt was covered in merit badges. He hadn't wanted to go out himself, but it was the last Sunday night of the month, which meant the free Senior Citizen Spaghetti Dinner at the KC. He was a regular volunteer but was afraid with all the craziness going on, other volunteers might decide to stay home. As it was, he had to turn in all his favors, even at eighteen, to get his mom to allow him to go. Once the dinner concluded, his mother's car wouldn't start, so he'd chosen to just ride the bus like his pre-driving days.

He leaned forward and looked down Pacific Grove Boulevard. Traffic was light, even for a Sunday evening.

Prey for the Damned

The bus was nowhere in sight, but he did see a television news van a block down.

He frowned. Journalism was not a career path he aspired to. He preferred a life of service. Maybe a minister or politician.

In the distance he saw bright emergency lights before his ears picked up the faint but growing sound of sirens. Less than a minute later, several police cars and an ambulance zoomed through the major intersection and past the bus top. A helicopter followed, like out of an action movie.

"Wow," Tobey said, the flashing lights finally disappearing in the west. He turned back to check for the bus and saw a small group of people fleeing from the shadows of Uno Street onto Pacific Grove. He heard them shouting, and he stood up, trying to make out what they were saying. The news van quickly raced away, passing the runners.

"What?" Tobey thought out loud, his mind whirling for a second or two, until he saw something where the news crew had been. He stepped out to the edge of the six-lane boulevard, peering at the abandoned camera lying on the pavement. They left the camera? Why?

Tobey's instinct to run kicked in a split second before the mob burst from the gloom of Uno Street. He turned and ran, following the sidewalk west. He ran several strides before glancing back, instantly wishing he hadn't. The mob spilled out on the major thoroughfare like a nightmarish dam break. The collection of people was strange and frightening. Instead of a pack of angry men, the mob was made up of little kids and the elderly, wearing savage, feral expressions. They moved quicker than they should. Almost jittery and frantic. Tobey didn't want to be caught by them, so he ran faster.

177

He sprinted along the boulevard for half a minute, his lungs just beginning to burn, when instinct caused him to throw another look over his shoulder.

The mob had spilled into the street, filling the eastbound lanes. Some had veered off across the concrete center divider. They were coming. Coming for him.

The sight was terrifying, but the realization of his imminent demise caused his thoughts to swirl, shatter, and explode. He continued down the sidewalk, his heart pounding against his sternum, fighting to be free of his ribcage as his legs fled his pursuers. Panting with every breath, he felt the wild, searing stares of the ones after him. Tobey wouldn't look back again. He was young and in great shape. He'd already earned all the physical fitness merit badges. But he wasn't in gym clothes, and running in dress shoes was less than ideal. Without thinking, he started The Lord's Prayer under his labored breath, but the words became jumbled with the lyrics of his favorite hip hop song. A faint police siren reached out to him.

Determined not to look back, he yelped as a drop of sweat invaded his eye. It was so strange. He could hear the faint footfalls of his pursuers, but nothing else. No shouts or screams of threatening profanity. The mob was dead silent. It didn't make sense, and it only made his living nightmare that much more terrifying.

Tobey's fear didn't allow him to feel the sidewalk under his feet. The police siren continued to gain in volume, but he ignored the temptation to pinpoint its location, though it was obviously heading in the same direction he was running and getting closer. In seconds the siren filled his ears, and to his left, the flashing lights of the police motorcycle were impossible to ignore.

The officer pulled up in the right-hand lane, her expression impossible to read behind the helmet's mirrored face shield. But before his mind could even contemplate a rescue, an old woman in a quilted robe and a little kindergarten-aged girl pulled the police officer from her cycle like a pair of cheetahs running down an antelope. The cop was gone, her motorcycle continuing forward until it clipped the curb and flipped up along the side of the road. Tobey veered off the sidewalk, unsure of where the cycle was going to end up.

"Holy shit," had just left his lips when he felt pain rake down his back, shredding the material of his uniform's shirt. The attack hardly caused him to break stride, but the sudden impact and weight on his upper back tossed him off-balance. Tobey was on the way to the ground, arms flailing, as something bit savagely into the side of his throat. He tumbled into the grass, his attacker small but powerful. He felt a small hand shoving his head to the side so it could burrow its head deeper into his neck. He coughed blood in place of a scream for help. Something was clawing open his shirt, and then the flesh of his chest. He shuddered as his body accepted the violation of a hand plunging inside him and—

His eyes rolled up into his head, showing white to the world as his heart was yanked free of his chest. The sounds of sucking and chewing escorted him from his death into the afterlife. The siren and lights on the police motorcycle continued to flash and wail, of no consequence to the horde of ravenous vampires on the rampage.

19

CALIFORNIA-STYLE BBQ

Moon sat in the parking lot of the Pearls' hangout, adjusting the AM tuner in her El Camino. The major news stations were broadcasting redundant emergency messages. Crazy Mabel tapped a knuckle on the half-closed driver's window. A pair of police cruisers raced by, sirens blaring.

"Anything?" Mabel asked.

Moon shook her head, continuing to adjust station to station with similar results. "Everything has gone to emergency broadcast. Can't reach my mother or grandmother either. Makes no sense this time of night."

Moon looked at her right hand. "Tonight is worse than last night. Sirens have been nonstop. Chaos all around us. Closing in." The Pearl leader switched off the radio and pulled the keys from the ignition.

"What're we going to do?"

Moon looked at Mabel as she stepped out of her vehicle. She wished she had an answer. She'd tried to contact Crater and Bam but only got their voicemail. Neither had called her back. Moon didn't like what she was feeling. The dread. The merciless darkness seeping out of every shadow, reaching out with murderous tendrils, their simple mission to seek out every opening of her body, invade her, and bring her life to an end in a cold and bottomless pool of absolute blackness.

She preferred to imagine drowning in inky, evil goo than being torn apart by soulless, bloodsucking vampires. If it was real. If it really could be real.

An older SUV pulled into the parking lot and jerked to a stop by the metal garage door entrance. The headlights flashed off and the front doors pushed open. Two of the Pearl sisterhood stepped out, the braided redhead, Lava, and the muscular Latina, Chili.

The redhead stepped up and immediately began to report. "It's crazy all over town. Total mayhem. The power's out in half the city. We didn't see a lot of cops."

Chili opened the passenger side rear door. Moon suddenly had a sick feeling, watching as Chili helped unload a handful of small children. There were three little girls and two boys. None looked older than kindergarten aged. Their faces were pale, with empty expressions. Their hands, faces, and clothing were stained with what Moon had to guess was dried blood. None displayed any obvious wounds, which made the stains even more unsettling.

Wearing a Dodgers ball cap, one of the girls clutched tight to Chili's leg as if her life depended on it. Her tiny face was buried in the faded denim.

"We drove by the twenty-four-hour daycare over on Marine. The lights were on, the front doors were wide open, and these kids were in the dark playground, sitting on the equipment." Lava leaned in and dropped her voce. "We couldn't leave them. There were dead bodies just inside the entrance. We tried to drop them off at the police station and then the hospital ER, but it was totally insane at both."

Moon stared at the children, uncomfortable with this unexpected development. "Take them inside, clean them up. Get them something to eat."

Chili nodded and coaxed them into the building. The kids did as they were directed, but none made eye contact or said a word.

"They look traumatized," Crazy Mabel said, watching and then following them inside.

Moon pursed her lips and shook her head. "You all did what you had to," she told her underling. "Thanks for going out and scouting around. TV and radio aren't saying shit about what's happening. We're on our own."

Lava nodded, and Moon patted her on the shoulder as she headed inside.

Alone, Moon stood outside, watching, listening, and feeling as her instincts screamed at her to gather her gang and head to Pacific Grove. They could join up with the Waves, have strength in numbers, and either ride out or fight their way out of what was coming. Since Breeze instituted the peace treaty for all the South Bay territories, her Pearls were not nearly as battle tested as they'd been four, five years back. If a bloody war was on their doorstep, most of her girls weren't ready for life or death combat. Moon fought to ignore the pull of her car, just steps away. She could be gone in seconds, safe behind the wheel, the percentages of her survival headed in the right direction. Of course, deserting her Pearls wasn't an option. Then again, neither was dying.

Moon's fear slithered around in a lazy circle and then lay in the pit of her stomach, heavy and cold. This sitting around doing nothing, knowing even less, was driving her crazy.

It didn't help that Breeze wasn't running the show. Sure, she trusted Bam and Crater, but Breeze was the magic man. The bigger the trouble, the tougher the challenge, the Wave leader always rose to the occasion.

She stared into the unusually light traffic and let her gaze lift into the star-filled sky. Tomorrow morning she and the Pearls would go out to breakfast and then take the short trip to Pacific Grove.

Moon headed inside, the metal garage door closing. She needed to figure out where they could safely drop off those kids and then try to get some rest.

When the metal door slammed shut, a chilling wave of finality coursed through her. Moon headed up the wide steel stairs to her private rooms behind the old operations room, two floors above what used to be the manufacturing floor. Mabel and Lava were straightening up a card table when Moon passed through to her quarters. The Pearl leader didn't feel like chasing sleep tonight, but she had a feeling a good night's sleep wasn't in the cards.

Moon slipped under the cool sheets, turned off the light, and closed her eyes. She quietly whispered her bedtime prayer, lightly tracing a fingertip over a variety of scars. It was a routine she'd started in the hospital after her accident. It calmed and reminded her of who she was as a warrior and a woman. Tonight she finished with a deep exhale and stared into the darkness of the ceiling. Her petite body relaxed, but her mind wouldn't be still.

Normally a good sleeper, Moon tossed and turned, troubled, panicked thoughts hellbent on keeping her subconscious occupied. Shadowy creatures stalked her along the shoreline while an arctic wind blew in from the ocean.

Moon sat up, both hot and chilled. She tossed off the covers, chest heaving in the inky darkness. Break-of-dawn light peeked through the blinds at the edge of her vision. For the first few moments she could only hear her heart pounding, but then the silence of her surroundings filled her ears. For a split second she felt safe, and then a bloodcurdling scream pierced the brick walls of the ex-manufacturing building. Instinct took over, and she turned on the bedside lamp and grabbed her magnum Derringer from under the other pillow. There was no time for pulling on clothing—her usual oversized T-shirt and silky boxers would have to do.

She burst through the apartment's front door and out into the playroom where she'd left Mabel, Lava, and Chili settling in to play cards. The folding table was vacant, one of the chairs lying on the floor. Moon pushed through the glass safety doors and down the long metal staircase to the main floor. Sounds of a commotion were coming from the bunkroom.

The lighting in the dorm was dimmed for nighttime, but Moon slapped at the light switches as she entered.

Crazy Mabel shouted her name. "Moon!"

The Pearl leader saw the statuesque enforcer across the chamber, her expression a shifting blend of fear, anger, and remorse. Moon took several hurried steps but suddenly stopped. A Pearl was sprawled on a lower bunk, her eyes staring into the upper bunk. Her throat was smeared with blood. Her face was drawn and pale.

Moon dropped to a knee and shook the young woman. "Sky! Sky!" It only took a moment for Moon to realize she was dead.

"Everyone's dead," Mabel called to Moon.

Moon stood and slowly took in the room. The dorm was far from full, with several no-shows the last couple of nights. Some of the membership had chosen to stay close to home and watch out for their families, but many hadn't checked in.

A dozen or so Pearls used the dorm last night. There was no movement from any of the occupied beds.

Lava called out from the far corner. "Over here!"

Mabel joined Moon as she wove her way across the chamber. They found the redhead kneeling.

"I've got blood," she said, her hand waving down the aisle.

Moon saw the trail of droplets leading down the smooth concrete floor. At the end of the aisle was a storage room the gang used for a variety of personal and membership items.

Lava stood, a large kitchen knife gleaming in her hand. Moon nodded toward the storage room, Mabel taking the lead.

As they grew close, they could see the door wasn't completely closed. The room beyond was dark.

"Trap?" Mabel hissed quietly.

"Don't fucking care," Moon said, stepping forward and kicking the heavy door. Lava ducked in and out, quickly turning on the room's lights.

Mabel entered, her gun aimed head high. Moon was on her heels, stepping around her to keep from colliding with her right hand.

"Fuck fuck fuck," Mabel whispered, the barrel of her gun dropping with disbelief.

Moon stared, not immediately understanding what she was seeing.

185

Lying about the floor of the storage room were the children Chili and Lava had rescued from the daycare. In their midst was Chili's blood-soaked body. So much blood, and her chest wasn't moving. The children were curled up, some sucking on their thumbs, some staring while in their unnatural slumber. One had lost his shirt, his torso covered in dried rivulets of blood, his pale stomach swollen like a well-fed tick.

Moon crept forward, her Derringer aimed dead at the forehead of the closest child.

"Hey," she barked, ready to pull the trigger. None of the child vampires stirred. Moon's gun hand trembled, taking all her resolve not to blow the head off the one in her sights.

"Get Chili," she whispered, holding her aim as Mabel and Lava grabbed their friend's legs and dragged her out of the storage room.

"Get the gas cans," Moon ordered, feeling the eyes of the women on her back. "Now."

The Pearl leader didn't move a muscle until she heard the women return and set down the metal gas cans. Moon backed out of the room, handed her weapon to Lava, and took a five-gallon container back in. She soaked all the shelves and file boxes until the container was empty. She tossed the dry can out of the room, the empty rattle echoing through the dormitory.

Moon grabbed the other large container out of Mabel's hand and stalked back into the storage room. She splashed a ring of gasoline around the children and then stood over each one, soaking their clothing and bodies, expecting them to suddenly jump up and attack her, their talon fingernails and viper fangs slashing and ripping, drinking the liquid life coursing through her veins. As the second container grew lighter, her heart pounded, surprised and thrilled to still be alive. Moon was amazed the little monsters didn't stir at all as she doused them.

"They're not fucking human," Moon hissed. "They slaughtered our sisters! They don't get to walk away because they're wearing SpongeBob pull ups."

Crazy Mabel continued to shake her head and mumble a string of profanities under her breath. Standing just outside the open doorway, Lava turned her back toward the room as Moon emptied the second container right up to the room's threshold.

"Did Chili still have her lighter?" Moon asked as she tossed the second can away.

Someone pressed Chili's bloody zippo into her hand. Moon pulled the storage door shut and slipped the deadbolt into place. The last splash of gasoline was just outside.

Moon flipped the lighter open, producing a nice flame. Nose wrinkling, she stared for a few seconds, a myriad of black thoughts swirling through her head.

"Fuck you," Moon said, dropping the lighter, igniting the gas. A few seconds passed, and then a loud whoosh sounded from the other side of the door. The vampire children began to wail like demons suffering in the darkest, dankest pit of hell. Heavy thuds came from the other side of the door, the kids ramming themselves against it, desperate to escape.

"When this is over, we pack a bag and head to Pacific Grove. We'll camp with the Waves until this is all over. Mabel, send a text to everyone with the plan in case some strays can make it on their own."

"On it," Crazy Mabel replied, sticking her gun into her waistband and pulling out her phone.

"Lava, pack up as much firepower as we can carry. We'll take my car."

The redhead nodded and jogged off through the dorm.

Moon stared at the storage room door, the wailing on the other side rising and falling. The weight of all the deaths moistened her eyes. Her mind rattled off a roll call of the Pearls who'd lost their lives: Vivian and Coco and Diamond and Petra and Kimbo and Sunshine and Bond Girl and Circus and Face Card and Zebra and Cheesy. Those little fuckers had literally torn the heart and soul out of the Pearls in a few deadly hours.

She hadn't taken the situation as seriously as she should have. Those little monsters had walked right into their clubhouse and fed on her second family. She'd opened the door and invited them in.

Moon was still staring at the door long after the screaming stopped, the smell of cooked flesh hanging in the air like the aroma of a hellish barbeque.

20

HIGH SCHOOL REUNION

Breeze was surrounded by cool darkness. He couldn't tell if he was inside or outdoors, though there was no starry sky or wind across his face. The absence of light was not foreboding or scary. It just ... was. Nothing for his senses to latch on to. No images, no sounds, no smells. It was like being in an empty jar with the lid screwed on. It didn't feel like he was floating, though he couldn't really feel the ground beneath his feet. He was just in this purgatory, waiting ... waiting ...

A faint sound registered, but his mind didn't recognize the source. His oddly comfortable surroundings didn't change.

The piercing blare of a car horn jerked Breeze out of his shallow doze. He scrambled to his feet, dropping the tire iron. The sun hadn't completely cleared the horizon, but the sky was clear. Shirtless, he was outside the garage's main entrance.

A car pulled up to the gate. It took a moment to recognize it. Moon's El Camino sat on the other side of the wrought iron bars, its engine grumbling quietly. The tinted glass made it tough to see how many occupants were inside. He waved and then stepped back inside for the opener.

As soon as the gate rolled open, Moon's car pulled in and parked. Breeze watched as the Pearl leader, Crazy Mabel, and another Pearl got out.

As Moon approached him, she cocked her head. "Looks like we weren't the only ones to have a seriously fucked-up night."

Breeze rubbed his face and tried to shake the lack of sleep loose. "You have no idea," he said, leading them inside.

"Really?" Moon said. "We lost a dozen sisters to a handful of little kids."

Breeze's body sagged against a wall. "Timothy got to my wife and child. They're dead."

The Pearls were stunned.

"Your … child?" Moon asked.

Breeze stared at her with bloodshot eyes. "She was due any day."

Lava leaned against the desk, her hand brushing against the duffel Breeze discovered.

"Don't touch that!" he shouted, causing Lava to bounce off the desk.

Moon moved toward Breeze, but he waved her off. "It's … the guys …"

The Pearls looked at the duffel, not understanding.

"It's Bam … and the guys. Their heads."

Lava backed away as Crazy Mabel made the sign of the cross.

Moon looked at Breeze. "Bam is gone? Who else is … inside?"

Breeze shook his head. "I don't know. Maybe five or six. I couldn't make myself look."

Moon glanced around the office. An open box of disposal work gloves sat on the other desk. She pulled out a pair and started toward the duffel. "I know most of your guys. I'll take a look so you know for sure."

Mabel placed a hand on her shoulder but looked away.

Unzipping the duffel seemed to take an eternity. Moon took a deep breath and exhaled as she pulled the bag open.

Across the room, Breeze closed his eyes and felt his knees sag a little.

"Oh God," Moon whispered, using the small flashlight on her keychain to examine the contents of the duffel. "There are ... seven, but I can't make them all out. I'm going to have to take some out."

"Jesus Christ," Mabel said, her face twisted with disgust.

Breeze couldn't close his eyes tight enough, trying his best to ignore the subtle sounds from across the room. The rustling of the duffle bag made his stomach twist and knot. Someone was breathing shallow and fast. Mabel had started praying and was listing out the names of her Pearl sisters lost during the night.

Outside, a small car horn beeped. Breeze ignored it.

"Hey, there's a security car out at the gate," Lava said. "It's pretty tore up."

Moon let out a deep breath. The next thing Breeze knew, Moon's cool hand covered his. "Bam, Crater, Sailor, Longstreet, Surgeon, Whisper, and Zero."

The car horn beeped again.

"Breeze, you got company," Lava said, peering out the window.

Breeze handed the gate opener to Moon, who tossed it to Mabel.

"Check it out. Friends, not foes. If you're not sure, end them."

191

Mabel nodded, pulling her pistol from her waistband. She glanced at Lava, who followed her out the door.

"Look at me," Moon's voice directed.

Breeze's mind was working through the seven Waves the Pearl leader had accounted for.

"Look at me," she repeated. Her tone was low and controlled.

Snippets of great memories flashed in a shuffling series of snapshots. So many good times-

"Look at me!" Moon shouted, shoving him in the chest.

Breeze opened his eyes just as the front door swung open. Emotion blurred his vision. And then Cheyenne ran into him so hard she almost took him to the floor. She threw her arms around him and squeezed so tight he couldn't breathe.

"Wally," she wailed, her tear-streaked face pressed into his chest. Her hair smelled of sweat and spoiled honey. He quickly swiped at his eyes and found himself looking straight into her sister Janice's angry expression.

"Breeze's ex," Mabel explained with a shrug.

"No shit," Moon said, stepping back from the pair.

"She could use a shower," Lava pointed out. Moon didn't disagree.

"Will someone tell me what the hell is going on?" Janice said. "The city is insane. My sister has turned into some kind of junkie overnight, and all she'll talk about is vampires, some guy from high school named Timothy Doleman, and Lancelot here."

Janice looked Breeze in the eye. "By the way, your armor isn't looking too shiny this morning."

Moon jumped up, spitting venom. Her face was nearly a foot beneath Janice's. "Back up! You don't want to be here, get the fuck out!"

Janice started to respond, but her eyes darted to the gun stuffed in the waistline of Moon's jeans.

Moon smiled like a hungry apex predator. "Make a move, bitch."

A moment or two passed, and Janice eased back a step. Then another. Her expression still displayed anger, but common sense won out.

"That's right," Moon whispered.

"It's been a hard night for everyone," Breeze spoke, literally forcing Cheyenne to release him.

Janise stepped forward to hug her sister.

Breeze said, "I have a plan, but I need more information. Doleman has the upper hand because he seems to have access to our personal information. Between that and this crazy vampire invasion, we're lucky to still be alive."

"Timothy has that edge because of me." Cheyenne sniffled. "He's in my head, so he knows what I know."

"So he knows you're here right now?" Crazy Mabel asked.

Cheyenne shook her head. "I don't feel him ... I think he's asleep. The Master tends to make everyone sleep when he does. Usually starting around dawn."

"The Master?" Breeze asked. "I didn't think Doleman was in charge."

"He's the Master's right hand. The plan is for him to lead the Master's army," Cheyenne explained.

Breeze took in the information, letting it roll around in his mind.

"Doleman can get in your head," the Wave leader started, "but can you get in his?"

Cheyenne looked at her ex, unable to stop the slight trembling. Her hand floated to her face. "I can. But it's so dark and twisted. His thoughts are filthy. Foul."

Moon stared out the office window as if the morning sun was streaks of gold. She slowly turned toward Cheyenne. "This Doleman. Was he the one Bam and Crater were trying to hide you from?"

Cheyenne dropped her eyes and nodded.

"Why is he after you?"

Breeze spoke up. "He's obsessed with her. Apparently since high school. Same with me."

"So we can use her to get to him," Crazy Mabel said.

"But it's not just him. We have to take out the Master. Cut the head off the snake," Breeze said.

"I know where to find him," Cheyenne said. "He's in the sub-basement of the Bastion Theater, but the place is full of vampires."

"The Bastion, huh?" Breeze paced around the office. Moon stopped him as he passed.

"Are all the Waves dead?"

He fired back. "Are all the Pearls?"

"Actually, no. A few are still alive. I didn't think our spot was safe, so they'll be here when they can."

Breeze relaxed a little. "Good. We'll need all the help we can get."

"And what about your guys? Have you tried to reach out?"

Breeze shook his head. "I was trying to keep them out of it. Do it on my own. And then I found the duffel bag." He paused and looked around the office. All eyes were on him. He took a deep breath and then let it out slowly. As the air leaked out, his response took a different direction.

He dug his phone out of his pocket. "We're going to use the day to regroup. We need to eat and rest and get our strength before sunset. I'll reach out to the rest of the Waves and see who's left. Janice, you up for a food run?"

Cheyenne's sister shrugged but didn't say no.

"Moon, you think your girl can go with Janice? There's a café about three blocks down. Just grab some breakfast combos or something."

Moon nodded, and Lava moved toward the front door.

"What if they're closed?" Janice asked.

"Do the best you can," Breeze directed. "It's daytime, so it should be safer, but no telling what's out there."

Lava showed Janice her weapon for reassurance. Janice looked unsure but followed the Pearl.

Mabel followed them, opening the gate.

Moon watched Breeze select the first contact. "We're going to end them, get our revenge."

Breeze glanced at Cheyenne. "You need to get some rest. But first, I need you to tell me something about Doleman we can use against him, okay?"

"Yes," she replied. "I want him dead."

"Well, he wants you alive, but the rest of us are on the clock."

"That's not true. Timothy doesn't want you dead," Cheyenne explained. "He wants you broken and then made into his slave."

"How the fuck could he make that happen?"

"The same way as me. Bite you, make you addicted to being fed on. Eventually you'll do whatever he wants."

"That's crazy," Breeze said. "A vampire bites you and you become a vampire, right?"

Cheyenne shook her head. "There are different kinds of bites. Bites to feed. Bites to kill. Bites to feed and turn."

195

Breeze let her words sink in. "So him not wanting me dead gives me an edge. What else?"

Cheyenne frowned. "I don't know."

"Think," Breeze pressed. "There must be something. Some detail, something he's afraid of …"

She closed her eyes, searching. Suddenly her eyes flew open and she smiled. "He's always been afraid of the water. He almost drowned at a friend's birthday party when we were seven or eight. His father drowned shortly after his mother passed away."

"Can a vampire drown?" Moon asked.

Breeze let the idea roll around in his head. "Don't know. But we can use it."

The Wave leader started texting. When he was finished, he sent it to every Wave in his contacts. *Time to get this party started.*

THE FINAL PIECES OF THE PUZZLE

Janice and Lava made it back with food half an hour later, the delicious and surprising smell of burgers, fries, and onion rings wafting through the office. They'd somehow convinced the cook to hook them up with a super-early lunch. Apparently, the usual Monday morning breakfast rush was nonexistent.

Breeze was just about to unwrap his double cheeseburger when his phone pinged. It was a text from Jim/Joe. He'd driven his mother and sister to Big Bear during the night and would be back this afternoon. Breeze's heart felt lighter knowing one of his brothers was safe.

Halfway through his burger another text came. It was from Jester. It was ominous. Only three letters.

alv

Breeze stared at the screen so long that Moon eased the phone from his hand and took a look.

"What do you think it means?" Breeze asked.

"I think it means alive." the Pearl leader said.

She gave him back the phone and Breeze called him. Each unanswered ring caused a little more anxiety. At the moment Breeze was sure it was going to voicemail, someone picked up.

No one spoke for a few seconds.

197

Finally, "Jester?" Breeze asked. The silence continued for another long beat.

"Breeze?" A sickly wheeze hung in the air.

Breeze wasn't sure it was real. It sounded like his name had been spoken by a ninety-five-year-old with malignant lung cancer.

"Jester?"

"They … got my family. Everyone." The long breath carried out like a death rattle.

"Jester, are you okay? Where are you?"

"Home, man. Home."

"I'm coming." Breeze said and hung up. Everyone in the room was locked on him. He stuffed his phone into his pocket and took another bite of his burger.

"Jester's in trouble. I'm going to Gardena for him."

"I'll go with you," Moon said. "Mabel and Lava can guard the gate while we're gone."

"No worries," Crazy Mabel said.

Breeze nodded and finished his meal. He felt Cheyenne's stare burning.

"You need to get some rest," he said, barely able to make eye contact. "You're gonna need your strength for what's coming."

Cheyenne took another fake nibble from her hamburger. Her fries and drink were untouched. She had the appetite and dark, hollow eyes of an addict.

Breeze's mind kept chasing itself, darting to and fro for a spark of a plan, but a solid direction avoided him. Right now, the plan was simple. Help Jester.

***

The ride to Gardena was quiet. Moon teased at the idea of driving the Mustang but settled for driving her own car. Breeze watched the world go by out of the open front passenger window, his arm hanging outside the door. It was another beautiful Southern California day, the blue cloudless skies stretched out over the ocean.

Breeze watched the world go by at seventy-five miles an hour and then forty-five once they left the freeway. When they pulled up in front of the duplex where Jester and his large brood lived, Breeze's arm's-length approach to the drive suddenly reversed itself. When Moon put her vehicle in park, Breeze took in the quiet stillness of the neighborhood. Very little traffic was moving in the blue-collar area. No dogs barking, no school buses. It was quiet and still.

Moon checked her gun. "Just in case," she said.

Breeze didn't blame her. Walking up to the front door, he noticed all the blinds were drawn despite the sunny day. Not right for a beach- and surf-loving Samoan family.

"I'm not sure you should go in," Breeze said as they stepped onto the small porch.

"I'd be happy not to, except you'd be extremely outnumbered. Especially if they're not themselves anymore."

The two gang leaders looked at each other until Breeze shrugged. "Suit yourself."

He pushed the doorbell and heard it ring inside the two units renovated into a singular six-bedroom, four-bathroom home. When no one answered, he tried the door. It was unlocked. He pushed it open. The shadowy gloom was not inviting. The inside of the house was uncomfortably hot, almost oppressive. A cloying odor of something unpleasant hung in the dry staleness. Breeze blew out a breath in preparation for whatever was to come.

"Jester?" Breeze called out, not in a big hurry to cross the threshold.

"Breeze." Moon's voice was pure warning.

Straight down the entryway hall, a small figure stood. Breeze tried to manage the gloom, to little success. It was a young girl, maybe seven or eight. Dark straight hair flowed well past her shoulders. She wore a long white T-shirt like a nightgown. Dark stains discolored the curve of the crew cut down to her midsection. Breeze suddenly struggled with the names of Jester's sisters. He wanted to call out her name, but it wouldn't come to him.

"Breeze," Moon whispered.

The girl snarled.

The hair on the back of Breeze's neck stood straight and tall like a guard at Buckingham Palace. "Crap," was all he could manage as the girl started running toward him.

Moon was suddenly in front of him, pulling her gun free. But before she could take aim, the girl veered into the darkness of the living room.

There was subtle movement inside the room to their left. It all happened so fast Breeze's heart didn't have time to quicken from fear. He glanced at Moon and then in the living room.

"Jester?" he called again, finally taking a cautious step in.

"Breeze." The voice was hardly recognizable. The wheezy tone made Breeze hesitate a moment before stepping into the large room.

In the far corner a small lamp cast the only light. The wide-bodied Jester was standing between it and Breeze, one hand pressed against his throat. Shadow-cloaked figures of various sizes stood and sat around the room. All were impossibly still and silent. He felt their wanton gazes on his skin. For a moment, Breeze was aware of the blood pulsing beneath the skin of his throat. He suddenly felt exposed and vulnerable. He might as well be naked and standing on an auction block in front of a room of faceless bidders.

An awful, unnatural whistle came from Jester's direction. It sounded like air passing through a ruptured lung. And then Breeze realized it was coming from under his friend's hand.

"An old woman knocked on the picture window. She was drenched in blood," Jester said, his voice so far from normal it made Breeze wince.

Moon stayed by the open front door, her hand resting on the gun stuck in her waistband.

"We let her in. A minute later and others forced their way in." Jester staggered forward a couple of steps. Breeze still couldn't make out his face.

"They were all so strong, so savage. They killed Mom and Dad and then fed on them. Fed on the rest of us, and left us to die, I guess."

"I don't think they left you to die," Moon said.

The subtle movement of Jester's head as if just realizing Moon was there was enough to make the Pearl leader fall back a step.

"I think she's right," Breeze said.

Jester slowly took in his siblings. "They … they turned us into … more of them?"

Breeze couldn't look his friend in the face. "These things killed my wife and baby and most of the Waves last night. We will get revenge."

"We will make them pay … for killing our parents, and my Wave brothers," Jester wheezed.

"Keep your phone on. I'm working on a plan."

Jester took another step forward, and Breeze was relieved he still couldn't clearly see the walking remains of his friend. "This will be our greatest victory. Our final war."

Breeze nodded, the intensity of his friend's stare unnerving. He backed slowly toward the front door. "Be ready." His instincts screamed that Jester's vampire family was going to rush him. Breeze's hands flexed into fists, not that it would have done him any good. He wasn't sure he could take Jester with a ball bat, and Moon probably didn't have enough bullets for all his siblings.

"I'm sorry," Jester said. The apology caught Breeze off guard. He paused his retreat.

"Sorry for what?'

"I can smell you, your blood. It makes me hungry. I'm not sure … how long you can trust me."

Breeze frowned, not sure what the Samoan meant.

"Not sure when the urge to hurt you … will be too strong."

"I trust you enough that when the time comes, you'll let me know."

Even through the gloom from across the large room, Breeze could see the subtle nod from his Wave brother. The tiny acknowledgement was good enough for him.

———※———

When he pulled the front door closed, part of him urged him to run to the car. Moon hadn't hesitated. She'd turned and ran to her El Camino, grabbing at the driver's side hood to keep her momentum from carrying her out into the deserted street. She jumped behind the wheel, slammed the door, and locked it like she was starring in a horror film. Breeze walked quickly after her, his instincts blaring at him to not turn his back on the front door. He slid in the passenger side and glanced back at the house. The living room picture window curtain parted enough for someone to look out. Breeze nodded and Moon's car pulled a tire-squealing U-turn and sped back down the street.

"Just when you think nothing can make you piss yourself," Moon said, her hands clenched on the steering wheel. "Why didn't they attack us?"

Breeze shrugged. "I don't know. They must not be fully turned. But now we have some soldiers the bad guys won't see coming."

Moon nodded. "Sure, if they don't kill us first."

Breeze didn't respond.

———————

When Moon and Breeze pulled up to the garage gate, Jim/Joe was standing outside the office. He patted his front pocket and the gate opened. His weary smile was a sight for sore eyes. Breeze and Moon climbed out of her car and the Wave was all business.

"I picked up Ant. He's inside. The ladies are trying to get some rest."

Breeze and Jim/Joe shook hands and hugged. "Good to see you, boss."

"Good to see you both," Breeze replied.

"You got a plan?"

"Working on it." A thought struck Breeze. "Janice is an underwater photographer, right?'

Jim/Joe nodded. "She used to work with Sailor sometimes, shooting videos for tours, you know."

Breeze's spark of an idea almost made him smile. "Wake her. We need a boat. And a shark cage."

"We can use Sailor's boat," Jim/Joe said. He frowned. "Sorry. I know he's dead. And I know about the others too. Before the duffel bag."

Breeze looked at Jim as if his twin brother Joe was standing right there.

"A shark cage?" Moon asked as Jim/Joe moved toward the office.

"It's a start," Breeze said. He yawned. "I gotta get some sleep." He followed Jim/Joe inside.

Moon stared after the Wave leader. "Fuck that. I'm never closing my eyes again. Ever." Moon yawned, deep and loud. The sheer weight and loss and grief of the previous night bore down on her from the inside out. It was impossible to ignore the sudden drop in energy, and her body trembled at the thought of what they'd just been through at the open tomb of what had been Jester's home.

"Okay. Maybe a catnap." She hurried to catch up.

22

THE BEGINNING OF THE END

By late afternoon, everyone had had a chance to lie down and get some rest. Under the circumstances, sleep was in short supply, but a few hours of rest was better than nothing.

Breeze struggled to fall asleep like everyone else, but his mind did a good job of putting together pieces of a plan of action. It was a solid start. After everyone was up, he shared his thoughts with the group, and Moon helped fill in the cracks.

Breeze stepped outside to contact Jester. When he got the man's voicemail, he left a detailed message. Not hearing Jester's voice was a bit discouraging, but Breeze put on his leader's face when he told the others.

"Jester won't let us down," Breeze assured. Jim/Joe and Ant didn't seem sold, but they didn't argue the point.

"Everyone got their assignment?' Breeze asked.

There were no questions from the Waves or Pearls, but Cheyenne's sister, Janice, spoke up. "The ocean group might want to get an early start. I'm not exactly a seasoned boat captain, and we'll need time to reinforce the cage."

"If you can trust me, I can handle the boat," Ant said. "I'm not as experienced as Sailor, but I can get it done, no problem."

Janice smiled. "Thank you for volunteering."

"No problem." The Jamaican nodded, letting his accent flow.

"And Moon and Jim/Joe are with me. Cheyenne, you need to be at the Pacific Grove pier ready to go at sunset."

"I'd feel better if you were going to be there, just in case. No offense, Ant."

The Wave shrugged. "None taken. When things get ugly, there's only one cool Breeze. But me and the rest of the Buffy gang will have your backs."

"Timothy has to be out of the way for the rest of the plan to have a chance of working. I can't be in two places at once. You have the easier part. Use his obsession for you and his weakness against him."

"You make it sound so easy," Cheyenne said.

"You wanna trade places with me?"

She quickly shook her head. "No thank you. I'll choose the pier over the theater."

"Me too. And speaking of which, we need to get downtown early and do a little recon. Take care of the Master's watchdog while everyone is asleep and get ready for sundown."

"And we all meet back here when our parts are played out." Moon concluded.

"So funny," Crazy Mabel said. "When I was a little girl I used to dream about having a sunset wedding at the beach."

"Things go sideways tonight and you might become someone's bride," Jim/Joe said. "Not sure it'll be the honeymoon you'd want."

"Oooooh." Mabel smirked at whatever unpleasant thoughts flashed through her head.

Jim/Joe laughed and then looked around. "Joe just said, 'Timothy just keeps striking out.'"

Breeze and Ant smiled, but the statement fell flat for the rest of the room. Bewildered, Lava looked around the group.

"I'll explain on the boat," Ant offered.

23
WHEN THE OCEAN SWALLOWS THE SUN

When Timothy's blood-red eyes snapped open, for a moment he couldn't remember if his heart was supposed to be beating or not. Was he dreaming when the Master awakened his army? His mind was a dark slate. Not a single image haunted him from his off-switch unconsciousness.

Though the Master lay in his recliner just across the room, Timothy didn't feel the need to verbalize his thoughts. The Master was in his head, a spider reading the vibrations of snared prey. The Master nodded, giving his silent permission before Timothy asked. Timothy felt the ache at the back of his skull. Cheyenne was calling out to him over and over, pleading with him to join her. She was tired of trying to escape him and the insatiable want she'd been inflicted with.

"Fetch the girl one last time," the Master instructed, "and then tonight my army of the damned completes their domination of the core territory. Understood?"

"Yes, Master," Timothy answered mentally, fully understanding the importance of tonight. By sunrise both he and the Master would be satisfied with this night's harvest. Imagining Breeze failing to save Cheyenne or himself from his vampiric power nearly gave the ex-deli owner a hard-on.

"Your will shall be done." Timothy spoke out loud unnecessarily as he left the Master's chamber.

Even as he climbed the ladder to access the theater's main floor, he sniffled and shrugged at his wardrobe. He was wearing the same clothes from the night he'd accepted his deal with the devil. His smell was more from the dried blood and gore from his many victims, than the ripeness of stale perspiration. It wasn't that many days ago when he'd rushed to take a long hot shower and deposit some of his clothing in the deli's alley dumpster. The nauseating reek coming from him now made him smile. He smelled like death. Foul, ugly, undeniable death.

When Timothy reached the quiet street in front of the theater, he sprinted west. One of the best abilities of becoming a vampire was the unnatural physical gifts. A cat's night vision. Extraordinary strength. Enhanced movement and quickness. In high school, he was much better running the mile in PE than the sprints. Now, he could run through the shadows of Pacific Grove at better than Olympic sprinter speed. Cheyenne was waiting for him at the Pacific Grove pier. He'd be there in minutes.

He veered into the middle of Pacific Grove Boulevard, the traffic much lighter than normal as the vampire hordes' savage attacks had the beach community citizens hiding in their homes.

Timothy ran without effort, creating a breeze across his face. As he approached an intersection with a stoplight, he grinned and smiled and laughed out loud. He ran down the yellow dashes separating the lanes, slapping at car windows, shattering them as he passed. The green left turn arrow appeared, the opposing traffic veering across his path. The driver of the lead car didn't have time to react to Timothy as he flashed into the intersection, leaping over the white SUV and continuing down the avenue, car horns blaring at his back. A block blurred by. Then another. And another. He glanced over his shoulder. The intersection was a tangle of cars, none of which were pursuing him. Even if they did, what could they do with him? Citizen's arrest?

He ran through an older middle-class area, the scent of the ocean becoming more and more prevalent. Dogs barked as he flashed through their territories. Shadows grew as the sun vanished beneath the horizon. As he neared the coast, he caught glimpses of the dark Pacific Grove pier. With the recent wave of violence, city officials had temporarily pulled the plug on the pier's entertainment area. The absence of all the amusement park lights was strange, ominous. A week ago Timothy would have felt anxious going to the water without the welcoming pier lights. But now he was king of the jungle, with nothing to fear. He was the boogeyman, the demoniac clown, the shadowy figure that blinked in and out of sight inside the half-closed bedroom closet. All the things he grew up needing his parent's protection from now helped feed his blackening heart.

He veered onto Pacific Coast Highway, easily avoiding the sparse commuter traffic. With the pier closed, the entrance and exit lanes were chained off. Timothy hopped the chain and slowed to a casual stroll. The boardwalk was thick wooden beams beyond the parking lot throughout the remainder of the pier. Timothy hadn't seen another person since he entered. Authorities probably couldn't afford a police presence with the widespread mayhem of the previous nights.

A few more steps and Cheyenne came into view.

She stood at the end of the pier, her back against the metal pipe railing. She was facing him, but he wasn't sure if she could see him with the sun all but gone.

Several steps later, she called out to him. "Stay there, Timothy. I need to talk to you."

He took a couple more steps and stopped. Cheyenne casually placed a foot on the lower length of pipe fencing. Timothy was close enough to hear the ocean meet the pier and the shore. Her hair was pulled back in a tight ponytail. She was dressed in jean shorts and a white T-shirt knotted at the midriff. He tried to slip into her mind like a snake slithering through a pet door, but she was ready. Her thoughts were vague and dark like the ocean.

"Let's just talk, okay?"

"If you say so," Timothy said, taking another step forward.

Cheyenne seemed to acknowledge his step by perching herself onto the top of the fence.

Timothy raised a hand in warning. "What are you doing?"

"I always thought you were a good guy back in high school. Kinda quiet, but decent."

"But not good enough. Not as good as Breeze."

She laughed. "No one was as good as Breeze. Every girl at Pacific Grove High School wanted to be with him. Some of the moms too."

"You never really gave me a chance."

"I never gave a lot of nice guys a chance, even before Breeze moved to town. I think part of me was waiting for someone like Wally."

The wind off the Pacific Ocean chilled Timothy's cheek. The sensation made him realize something was wrong. Cheyenne had lured him there for a reason.

"I knew you liked me, but a lot of boys were sniffing around me, especially as I filled out. I never disliked you, Timothy. I just never paid enough attention to you."

Instinctively, Timothy took in his surroundings. If this was a trap, the concept was beyond him. Whatever it was, it had no chance of working. But still, something was off. While the sound of the ocean was calming to many, it set his nerves jangling.

"You seem ... hesitant. Worried." Her words had an underlying strength.

Timothy slowly stuck out his hand. "Why don't you come down from there? Whatever your plan is, it's not going to work, especially without Breeze."

"He has somewhere else to be." Cheyenne felt the nudging at her thoughts and instantly concentrated on the ocean beneath her. "Are you afraid of the water?" she asked with a quizzical tilt of her head.

Timothy took another step, his hand beckoning. "Please come down."

"You know Breeze will never let you have me."

"I can make you come down." He didn't like her composure any more than his proximity to the water.

Cheyenne smiled like a woman with the world's greatest secret and then pushed away from the railing.

Like a Praying Mantis catching a fly, Timothy caught her. He stood on the top of the pipe railing, one hand clutching her ankle. A split second later he lost his balance and fell, following Cheyenne through the darkness toward the water. It happened so fast and unexpectedly he hardly had a chance for his fear to manifest into a yell.

When he hit the water, his fear exploded. The ocean subdued his movements, blinding him and pouring into his mouth, cutting off his cries. He thrashed about, losing his grasp on Cheyenne. The more he tried to scream, the more water filled his throat and lungs. He couldn't tell which direction was the surface, and despite his enhanced strength, his arms and legs felt heavy and clumsy. He clawed at the cool water surrounding him and then at his throat as his mind began to swirl into nothingness.

Could a vampire drown? Is this what his father felt as he succumbed to the ocean's power?

Timothy found out the hard way.

Ocean water gushed from his mouth as his body spasmed back to consciousness. Disoriented as his blurred vision fought to right itself, the world was topsy turvy. It was dark, but his night vision made out the metal bars surrounding him. It took Timothy a moment to recognize he was hanging upside down, with hard restraints around his ankles and wrists. He belched up more water, his chest heaving as he forced his lungs to clear. The sound of the ocean filled his ears, along with a boat's engine.

"Wakey, wakey," a male voice said.

As his vision cleared, he could see he was facing away from the boat, looking through the bars of some sort of cage hanging over the ocean's surface. They were a great distance from shore. If not for his enhanced vision he probably couldn't have seen land.

"Sadly, we're going to make this quick," Ant said from the rear deck of the boat. "You're in a titanium polycarbonate shark cage. Your ankles are double cuffed to the bars, and your wrists have been tripled cuffed, along with a shitload of zip ties. We weren't sure if you could drown or not, but it was worth a try. If nothing else, you'll pass out and be trapped until the saltwater softens the meat off your bones so the smaller fish can nibble on it. Knowing how much you like the water, Breeze thought it was the perfect way to end your fucking ass."

As the words sank into the vampire's mind, Timothy's fear overwhelmed him. His scream accompanied his futile struggle.

There was a smattering of chuckles from the boat.

"I guess that means he's ready to go."

"I'll get away. I'll break free, and find all of you. I'll slaughter your families. I'll kill everyone you've ever known and cared about!"

There was the sound of mechanical gears, and then the shark cage began to lower.

"Goodbye, Timothy." It was Cheyenne's voice, her tone cold and dismissive.

As the bottom of the cage broke the surface, Timothy's rage turned to fear. "Don't do this. Please. I'm sorry for everything I've done … please!" The ocean ended his pleading, swallowing his head and shoulders, causing his legs and torso to thrash frantically. The group on the boat watched as the cage slowly disappeared under the waves, and then Ant pulled a small lever and released it from the steel cable.

"That was almost too easy," Crazy Mabel said.

Cheyenne stood at the boat's rear, staring down into the ocean's darkness. She pulled the blanket tighter around her shoulders and whispered a prayer.

As the sun set in the deserted downtown section of Pacific Grove, Breeze strode through the growing shadows down the empty street toward the old movie theater. Dressed in his favorite jeans and his black and aqua leather Wave vest, he had to force himself to keep from smiling. He approached the small security car parked in front of the Bastion, a backpack strapped tightly to his shoulders. A few steps from the car, the familiar security officer squeezed out from behind the steering wheel. He stepped toward Breeze, reaching for his polished baton. Breeze let the smile spread across his face as he reached to the small of his back and pulled out the automatic. The look on the security guard's face as the bullet struck his forehead was almost comical. Breeze might have felt sorry for the man, who was as much a victim as any, but there was no time for pity or mourning. Just time for killing.

Breeze walked past the crumpled body, pausing to relieve the man of a large keyring and to make the sign of the cross.

"Sorry," he whispered.

He stood and took in the Bastion. Jim/Joe appeared from around the corner at the far end of the block. He sprinted down the sidewalk, pulling up right beside his leader.

"Joe wanted to race," he explained between breaths.

"Joe was always quick," Breeze said, handing over the keyring.

"You think the Master knows we're here?"

As if on cue, the two Waves heard a clicking sound from the theater's front doors.

"Guess that answers that."

"See ya when I see ya," Jim/Joe said, turning and running back the way he came. Halfway down the street he called back over his shoulder, "You smell wonderful!"

Breeze chuckled as he stripped off the backpack and pulled out a small mag-light. He was just about to turn it on when the Bastion Theater marquee blazed to life.

THEATER CLOSED.

Breeze stuffed the flashlight into his pocket and walked into the deserted lobby of the place where he and Cheyenne had first kissed. In a split second it seemed like yesterday and a long, long time ago.

As empty and still as the formerly grand entrance was, the Wave leader could almost feel the menace waiting for him beyond the heavy curtains separating the lobby from the theater. Instinct warned him to pause at the burgundy drape, but he didn't care enough to break stride. He pushed through the velvety curtain and froze. The theater house lights were on, and Breeze's breath caught in his throat.

Every seat of the Bastion was filled. Vampires crammed every aisle, including the one he stood in. The balcony was also packed full of the pale-faced creatures. Those closest to him shrank back, the stench of garlic wafting from him head to toe.

"Welcome," a young male voice called out from the theater's sound system. "I wondered if I'd get a chance to meet you while you were still you."

Breeze looked around, taking it all in while forcing himself not to make eye contact with any of the monsters.

"You don't really think the garlic is keeping them back, do you?" the voice sneered.

"I figured it couldn't hurt."

"Clever boy. I understand Timothy's great dislike for you."

"Funny—I always thought we were good. Guess I should have been paying closer attention."

"Mr. Thornton, could you spare me a few moments?"

Breeze shrugged. He had nowhere to go.

Suddenly, whatever invisible barrier was holding the creatures at bay was suddenly gone, and the sea of vampires surged. Breeze couldn't help but flinch, but he held his ground as the creatures rushed by him, hunger fueling their flight. Some eyed him like a juicy hamburger as they shouldered past him, but none attacked.

Breeze stood, jostled by the frantic contact. As full as the theater was when he'd entered, it took only moments to empty. Breeze couldn't remember taking a breath during the evacuation, but he exhaled as the last ones ran by.

"Feel better?" The Master's voice called out, surrounding him. "I wanted to give your suicide mission a glimmer of hope."

Breeze didn't move.

"Don't worry—your people out back were not touched. I'm all for fair play."

Breeze didn't have to wait long. Jim/Joe and Jester appeared at the far side of the stage. Breeze caught a glimpse of some of Jester's siblings. Jester didn't look good even at a distance. He appeared to be laboring; his chest was falling and rising too quickly.

"I'm in the basement beneath the stage. Last chance to survive the night, Mr. Thornton."

Breeze started down the aisle in an easy lope and then joined his Wave brothers on the stage. They found the wooden access door, and Jester summoned his family with a single head tilt.

The Wave leader lifted the hatch. He looked over the small female tribe. Jester's sisters all had a family resemblance. They were all island girl attractive, fit and strong. They had swimmers' shoulders and muscular thighs. Like Jester, dark circles hung under their bloodshot eyes, and their skin lacked its normal youthful luster.

"After you," Breeze said with a sweep of his arm.

The young ladies all looked to their brother. His encouraging smile failed miserably, but it was enough to start them moving below the stage.

Breeze was last to descend, right behind Jim/Joe. He'd just left the light of the theater behind when the stomach-flipping stench of rotting flesh, stale sex, and an overflowed toilet slammed into his midsection. One hand left the ladder to cover his mouth, but it was hardly enough.

Breeze flipped on his flashlight as his foot touched the floor, but he didn't need it. A dim, yellowish light came from a connected room. Jester and his family had already entered. Breeze's eyes watered from the horrid smell.

The Master, wrapped in a thick black robe, was relaxing in a lounge chair. All he needed to complete the picture was a cold beer and a local ballgame on the TV. Next to the chair was the savaged remains of a woman. She appeared Asian, stripped to a soiled pair of panties. The majority of her skin had been peeled away in long strips, revealing raw, angry flesh. Her face was exposed muscle and sinew, a nightmarish horror movie mask. If she hadn't blinked, one would have thought she was dead.

"Okay, the gang's all here—or at least what's left of it," the Master chuckled, pushing his thick, black-framed glasses up the bridge of his nose.

Jester and his sisters circled the recliner. Their ferocious anger was barely contained. Jim/Joe stood off to the side, smirking from a private joke. Breeze could almost imagine Joe standing next to his twin brother, giving him confidence.

Breeze felt the cold, silky nudging of the Master inside his head.

"Not much of a plan, really. Have me turn you, and then you use the power to kill me? Simple, but really lacking much imagination. I'm disappointed."

Breeze shrugged. "Complicated isn't always genius."

"Kill him!" Jester roared, and his sisters snarled and started forward. The Master's grin didn't even fully form before he seemed to have shifted position in his chair as he licked fresh blood from his fingernail talons.

The girls all wobbled and shook, and then they started falling to the floor, their heads either sliding off their shoulders to the concrete or flipping back on their shoulders like a hoodie, eyes staring lifelessly.

"Young women just taste so good." The Master cooed at the dark blood webbing his fingers.

Jester took in the results of the carnage as his sisters fell around him. He cried out, dropping to his knees in heart-rending defeat. He crawled from body to body, wailing. The skinned woman began to cry like a sick kitten.

"I'm quicker than I look."

Breeze fought to keep his composure. "Have you touched base with Timothy?"

The Master took his time enjoying the blood covering his hands. "Not since he left. Why?"

"He should be dead by now."

The Master stared at the Wave leader. He probed Breeze's mind and then chuckled.

"You can't kill a vampire by drowning. You'll have to try again."

"I'm planning on it. But I needed him out of the way to deal with you."

"Well, I'm ready whenever you are," the overweight teenage vampire master answered, completely comfortable in his chair.

Breeze shrugged off the backpack and unzipped the main compartment. He pulled out a large metal hammer and a homemade wooden stake.

The Master comically sniffed at the air. "Is that pine?"

Breeze chuckled. "You're not what I expected, even after Cheyenne filled me in. But you are a perverted, murdering motherfucker."

The Master flinched. "Ouch. If it weren't true, I'd be offended."

For a split second the Master appeared right behind Breeze but then returned to the recliner.

"Speed kills," the Master teased, batting his eyelashes.

"True," Breeze said. "I had to think hard about your real weaknesses. Eventually I had to go way outside the box."

The Master trembled slightly as if a chill had caressed his skin. Breeze clenched the hammer and stake and strode across the room. The Master smiled but didn't move. When Breeze stepped up next to the recliner, the goofy smile on the Master's face twitched. Breeze pressed the point of the stake into the Master's sternum. The smile disappeared as the creature found his body was not under his control.

Breeze's smile was relaxed. "I'll bet you didn't know I wasn't the clear-cut choice to lead the Waves."

"What? What did you do?" The Master's eyes widened, and the pitch of his voice raised with fear. The parlor tricks for the master vampire appeared to be over.

"Jim's twin brother, Joe, was pretty popular with the guys. Great guy. Tough as nails. The joke was I won the election to lead the Waves by one vote—Jim's. I guess they were fighting at the time."

Jim spoke up. "I love my brother, but I thought Breeze was the one and only. As usual, I was right."

"Joe died, and over the years, Jim has taken all kinds of shit about his brother, Joe, still hanging around. You feel Joe? He's the spirit possessing your body right now, bitch. I'll bet this stake is going to fucking hurt," Breeze said as he raised the hammer.

"Wait, wait, wait," the Master pleaded. "I'll … I'll give you Timothy's position as the head of my army. You'll have more power than you could ever dream of having."

Breeze shushed the Master like a newborn.

"Better hurry," Jim/Joe warned.

"Jester," Breeze barked out.

The Samoan brute bounded to his feet, grabbing the hammer and stake from his leader.

"Please … don't."

"I will … see you in Hell." Jester snarled, his eyes burning into the vampire's. The Master's deafening scream started just before the stake plunged through his chest.

The monster wearing the Master's flesh thrashed at the killing blow. The skin of his face split apart, and a mutant human bat face screeched in pain.

Breeze and Jester stumbled back from the recliner, the palms of their hands pressed against their ears.

The Master's body fell still, and inside his ill-fitting clothing his flesh dried and fell away from the bone, dust swirling in the air. For an instant, as the screaming died away, Breeze thought he caught a glimpse of Joe, adorned in his Wave leather vest, smiling peacefully as his form was whisked skyward. A split second later, nothing was left in the recliner but a big wooden stake punched through the middle of a black ash outline of what had been a master vampire.

The reeking chamber was silent. The should-have-been-dead woman whined softly on the floor for help. Breeze glanced over at Jim/Joe, who'd dropped to his knees and was staring above the chair.

"What happened?" Breezed asked.

Jim/Joe shook his head, a smile growing as his eyes moistened. "I don't know, but he's gone. Maybe he wasn't able to pull away from the Master. But I can feel his essence. His spirit is finally at peace."

Breeze wasn't sure what to say at the unexpected turn of events. He grabbed Jim's shoulder. "He saved our asses."

Jim nodded, sobbing softly.

Breeze forced himself to ignore his friend as he looked over at Jester, who was bent over the woman by the recliner. It took a moment to register and recognize the sound.

The sucking sound.

A trickle of fear ran up Breeze's back. "Jester?"

The big man froze, like a child caught nabbing a cookie. He slowly turned, dark blood and drool dripping from his chin. Jester snarled, and Breeze wished his gun was in his hand.

Jester pointed a trembling finger. "We were supposed to kill the Master *before* he killed my family. You had a plan." Suddenly Jester grabbed at his midsection and went down on a knee. He grunted and moaned in pain. Breeze wasn't sure what to do.

Help? Run? Kill?

A fourth option presented itself. He froze.

"Breeze," Jim warned from across the room, but it was too late.

"I'm hungry!" Jester screamed as he lunged toward Breeze.

Breeze blinked, shocked at his friend's sudden rage. Then Jester was gone.

Wait. Wrong.

Jester had moved much quicker than Breeze expected. The wide-bodied Samoan was now on top of him, his enraged face full of jagged teeth with the exception of the classic vampire fangs. Breeze had no physical answer for the assault. He threw his hands out, catching his friend around the throat, but it was like trying to stop a 275 pound pit bull. Jester was going for his throat, and there was no way to stop him. The more Breeze strained, the closer Jester's monstrous face got. Breeze felt his eyes growing large with dread. He was going to die.

The searing pain of Jester's bite only lasted a second and then stopped like a magic trick. Breeze felt his windpipe collapsing, crushed between Jester's jaws.

His hands, suddenly weak, fell away from Jester's throat. Breeze's eyelids fluttered, his eyes rolling back into the darkness of his skull. He felt Jester's heart pounding through his chest against his own.

No—it wasn't Jester's heart. It was his own, beating to escape the cage of his ribs as Jester's massive arms encircled his frame and crushed him in a grotesque embrace.

Breeze's mind was swirling down the drain of unconsciousness. There was no rush to his defeat.

Jester's scream was like the distant erupting of a volcano. Breeze wasn't sure the wail was real. He really didn't care.

Wallace Thornton was dying.

223

Wrong again. Wallace Thornton, aka Breeze, was dead.

———※———

Flashes of life danced like electrical shortages in his brain.

He thought he heard a familiar voice crying out. Jim?

There was pressure on his chest and then on his mouth. Something struck his face.

He felt his body jostling and then lifted.

At some point there were voices. Male. Female. Conversations were held, but his jumbled thoughts couldn't grasp them. Something soft and wispy covered his face.

Then nothing for a stretch of hours and hours. No sensory input at all. No dreams.

———※———

When Breeze woke up, he didn't know what day it was, but he sensed it was sunset. He could distinguish the scents of the people in the room. He was among friends but he couldn't move. Thick metal chains circled his body like pythons. His arms were pinned against his naked torso. Suspended in the air, he hung like a car engine. The garage lighting was dim.

A soft hand touched his foot, startling him. "Breeze?" Moon whispered.

The Wave leader tried to escape his chain cocoon, to no avail. He looked down at Moon and hissed like a cobra. He caught himself, closed his eyes, and tried to focus. Concentrating was difficult. He felt the oddest gnawing in his gut. He was empty and famished at the same time.

The oversized metal links pressed into his skin. He was completely naked under the chains.

"Bam! Crater! Let me down!" Breeze called out.

In moments, Jim and Ant joined Moon, along with the other surviving Pearl members, Crazy Mabel and Lava. Breeze took in the group, pushed uselessly against the chains again, and then relaxed.

"Jokes over, okay?" Breeze's expression melted into a sincere sorry for several seconds and then flared into white-hot fury. "Let me down," he demanded. "Let me loose!"

"Breeze?" Moon asked quietly. "We gotta talk to you."

Breeze got still and ignored the Pearl leader. He turned his head and focused on his high school sweetheart as she stepped into the garage.

"I can smell the blood coursing through your veins, Cheyenne. So hot and sweet. What are you—O negative?"

"Get her out of here," Moon ordered.

"I can smell Timothy swimming inside you. You're his blood whore forever."

Cheyenne started toward him, but Crazy Mabel forced her out of the garage.

The room was quiet for half a minute. Breeze looked confused. "Where is everybody?"

"Everybody?" Moon responded. "You mean the other Waves?"

"Everybody?! What's wrong with you?" He strained against the chains again. "Come on. Enough already. I need to call my wife."

A dropped pin would have sounded like a hand grenade.

Breeze's face clenched and he cried out.

"Your wife and child are dead," Moon explained. "So are most of the Waves. A lot of Pacific Grove's residents are dead. We think you're turning into a vampire."

Breeze screamed and strained to break free, his effort making his bound form dance at the end of the supporting chain. Moon and the others darted back, unsure of their safety. Profanity streamed from his mouth in English as well as Spanish. Spit flew from his mouth as he cursed the world. At some point Moon and the remaining Waves left Breeze alone in his own private hell.

24

WORKING ON THE CHAIN, GANG

Eyes beyond bloodshot with a complexion drained of human coloring, Breeze murmured like a man possessed by a ravaging fever through the night of his first return. Shortly after dawn, he quit mumbling and passed out.

The next sunset he awoke tormented and angry at his family and friends for allowing his soul to be taken and then deserting him. He ranted for about an hour, whispered about his gut-gnawing hunger for another hour, and then grew quiet for the rest of the night.

His third night was completely quiet. Concerned, Moon checked on him several times, afraid the unnerving quiet signaled he'd somehow gotten free. Each time she found him just hanging like a human ornament. His eyes were closed, and he didn't speak or react to her at all.

The fourth night, Moon startled awake from a half-sleep expecting Breeze to be looming over her in the shadows. He wasn't there, but Cheyenne's sleeping bag was empty. Moon took the gun from under her pillow and quietly moved toward the garage. Fighting off the instinct to turn on lights, she was not surprised when she discovered her with Breeze. She was kneeling close to his suspended

227

form, as if praying to him like Jesus on the cross. Moon listened, her fingers lightly tapping on her handgun.

"You know we need you. I need you," Cheyenne whispered. "I'll let you loose if you give me your word you'll only feed on me, and no one else."

Breeze's upper torso was in the deep shadows of the work bay's high ceiling. Moon couldn't see his face, and wondered if his eyes were open or not. Cheyenne reached out, almost touching his bare foot.

"The others don't know you like I do. They don't understand our bond. That you could never hurt me, vampire or not."

Breeze's chained form swayed the tiniest bit. The subtle movement was just enough to startle Cheyenne, who fell back on the concrete floor. From the darkness above her, Breeze laughed quietly, low in his throat. The hair on the back on Moon's neck stood up and she jerked the gun free of her waistband. Cheyenne bolted from the garage, nearly running the Pearl leader over. Breeze's ex- went out to her sister's car and didn't return inside until daylight. His chilling laughter stopped the moment Cheyenne stepped outside. When Moon returned to bed, there was no more sleeping. Breeze's laughter haunted her thoughts well into the next morning.

The fifth night he called out to Moon. When she, Jim, and Ant entered the garage, Breeze spoke softly. "Bring me some blood or kill me."

It sounded like Breeze talking, though a bit hoarser than usual. The teeth and fangs he'd grown impossible to hide. Somehow his bloodshot eyes didn't seem monstrous, more a symptom of his new condition.

"You kept me alive out of some sense of hope. At some point you're going to have to trust me," he said. "Trust me or kill me. You choose."

"Like you trusted Jester?" Moon said.

"I put him in a terrible spot. I didn't understand. I couldn't have." Breeze stared through the gloom into Moon's eyes. "But I do now."

Moon and the two Waves looked at each other.

"You're gonna have to let me feed so I can gain a sense of control."

"A sense?" Jim asked.

"If I can feed, I think I can better control the urge to feed and possibly kill you guys."

"Makes sense," Ant said. "I like not getting fed on."

"But the question is, how do we know for sure?" Jim asked.

Moon looked at the two Waves and shrugged. "We don't."

The garage was quiet as the trio thought it over. Breeze didn't bother trying to convince them.

"I have blood for you," Moon offered. Ant and Jim stared in shock.

"From the underground freakshow network. Blood worship is big."

"I gotta admit, you had me a little worried," Jim said, almost smiling. Moon left for the blood while Ant lowered his leader closer to the floor.

"Jester?" Breeze asked.

Jim shook his head. "I had to put him down. If I hadn't, he'd have killed me and the girl."

"The girl?"

"You know—the one on the floor, all torn up."

Breeze's head sagged a little. Jim continued.

229

"She asked me to, you know, take mercy on her. I did. The Bastion Theater had a suspicious fire. The security guard wasn't much help to authorities. Couldn't remember anything much after taking the job."

Breeze looked confused. "Didn't I shoot him? In the head?"

Jim smiled a little. "Rubber bullet put him down. You didn't want to kill him if you didn't have to."

Ant spoke. "And just so you know, we took the duffel bag with the guys to a local mortuary and had them cremated. No questions asked. We dumped the ashes off the pier last night. I kept the bag. Wasn't sure if you'd want it or not."

Breeze nodded at the news. Moon walked in holding some medical blood bags, a small screwdriver, and a kid's crazy straw.

"I'm not sure how this is supposed to work," Moon said. "Let's just start with one bag and go from there, okay?"

Breeze chuckled at the perversely bizarre situation. "I'm not even sure if I prefer regular or diet."

The joke caused everyone to relax. A little.

25

AND A SOGGY CHERRY ON TOP

Cheyenne set her basket of freshly dried clothes on her living room couch as the local ten o'clock news began. She started to switch the channel to music but changed her mind as the news anchor charged right into an unusual story.

"Good evening, South Bay. This is Melanie Sunday filling in for vacationing Drake Patterson. We start tonight's broadcast with a story fit for Hollywood studios. Local university filmmakers scouting offshore locations for their short thriller happened upon what was thought to be a submerged horror film prop a couple of miles off the Pacific Grove pier. When the students investigated closer, they discovered the subject shackled inside the shark cage wasn't a dummy, but a deceased male. The estimated length of time the man was submerged made identification extremely difficult. The cage was towed to shore and turned over to local law enforcement authorities to continue the investigation."

Cheyenne stared at the TV, absorbing the story. She slowly folded her laundry as the telecast continued. She finished organizing her clean clothes and then put everything away. She changed the channel and perked up at a favorite disco song. She danced her way around the room, hanging up items and tucking folded pieces into drawers. She danced her way back into the living room, singing the lyrics with loud bravado.

When the song faded, she noticed the living room wall clock. She had an early class, so it was time to turn in. She used the remote to turn off the TV and decided to leave the living room window open. Such a nice night.

Cheyenne stepped into the bathroom and peeled down her jean shorts and underwear to pee and then stopped at the sink to splash warm water on her face to help clear away her makeup. She patted her face dry and checked out her reflection. Her eyes were clear and sparkling. Her skin held a healthy tan from the beach. The nightmare from all those months ago was well behind her, and she looked it. She smiled at herself and turned out the light.

Cheyenne wandered into the bedroom, casually pulling off her sleeveless sweatshirt and tossing it into the empty laundry basket. She unsnapped the clasp of her shorts and let them shimmy down her hips to the hardwood floor. She used a bare foot to kick them into the laundry basket, her black sports bra seconds behind. Cheyenne hopped on her queen bed and then changed her mind and slid back down to the floor to kneel bedside to pray.

"Now I lay me down to sleep," she whispered, an innocent smile tugging at the corner of her lips. When the wafting of saltwater and putrid rot teased her nostrils, she ignored it and continued her prayer.

"You bitch," Timothy whispered from the bedroom threshold. His words sounded mushy; his tongue mostly eaten away by the ocean's tiniest fish.

Her back to him, Cheyenne did not react to his threat. She finished her prayer and climbed into bed without acknowledging his presence.

Timothy took a step into the room. His appearance should have been shocking. The time spent under the ocean waves wasn't kind to his lifeless-looking flesh. He and his tattered clothing reeked of rotted fish. His lipless smile was grotesque. "After I feed on you to get my strength, I'm going to make you do things—"

Suddenly Breeze was standing in front of him. His usual healthy beach tan was missing. He was sickly pale yet looked strong in his black leather Wave vest.

"What kind of things, Timothy?"

Timothy blinked, startled at his adversary's sudden appearance. Then Breeze was suddenly standing right behind him.

He whispered into the ragged hole that was once an ear. "I'll bet you didn't know when we sank you in that cage, we implanted a tiny tracker deep in your left ass cheek, just in case you survived and made it back to shore. I was hoping you would, and here you are."

Timothy blinked again and Breeze was back in front of him.

The Wave leader's expression showed concern. "You don't look too good, Timothy. Can I call you Tim? No?"

Timothy's mind was a touch slow from his watery imprisonment. He watched Cheyenne turn her back to him and curl up under the covers, catching her peaceful expression despite his intrusion.

"You're not quite the boogeyman you were back in the crazy vampire days. I'll bet you haven't had much luck reaching the Master."

Breeze was back behind him, whispering. "We killed him. Sorry."

Breeze appeared back in front of him. "Actually, I've killed all the other vampires in the Southland from the Master's army. Well, almost everyone."

Breeze's face wrinkled. "Do you have any idea how bad you smell? You could use some sun too, but you were never a real beach guy, were you? You burn way too easy, and your crazy fear of the water. You'd been better off in Hollywood as a goth guy."

Breeze turned and casually walked over to Cheyenne's bed. He took a seat on the corner of the mattress and grinned. "I can sense your weakness, Tim. Any last words?"

"My name is Timothy," the vampire answered. Timothy tried to smile. "Killing your wife and baby was the best night of my life."

Breeze was back in Timothy's face, his hands wrapped around his enemy's throat. His fingernails grew into talons, which slid into the soft flesh of Timothy's neck like a paring knife into spoiled fruit.

"I'm so glad you brought them up. I think about them just about as much as I've dreamed of these last moments with you. You stand about as much chance against me as my wife did against you. Maybe less."

Timothy blinked, and the realization of his pending doom passed through his ravaged expression. "Killing me won't bring back your happiness."

Breeze's smile was terrifying. "Oh, but you're wrong. Killing you is going to make me very, very happy for a long, long time. Say goodnight to Tim."

"Goodbye," she said, nestling into the covers. She didn't bother to roll over and open her eyes to watch.

"See you in Hell," Timothy said. He started to say something else but was cut off. His body sagged to the floor, while his head remained clutched in Breeze's hands.

His mouth yawned open as Breeze squeezed. Timothy's skull slowly collapsed, bones crunching as they gave way. Breeze watched the light go out of his enemy's eyes, his fangs showing as he smiled. He dropped the misshapen head to the floor and stared down at his revenge.

"Is it over?" Cheyenne asked, her back still to the scene.

"Oh yeah," Breeze said softly.

"Thank you," Cheyenne replied with a yawn, rolling onto her back "Would you like a little something for the road?" She tossed off the covers.

Breeze stared at her, her smile as inviting as her fit, tanned flesh. She turned her head away from him, and he watched the blood coursing just under the skin. One of her legs bent at the knee, and he could just make out the healed wounds on her inner thigh. For a moment he wondered if all predators looked at their prey the same way. He returned her smile and moved toward the bed, managing to not lick his lips.

Breeze carried the large, stained duffel bag out of Cheyenne's building. Moon was waiting behind the wheel of his vintage Mustang. He tossed the bag into the trunk.

"He's dead?" she asked.

"Like disco."

"The slaughterhouse?"

"I was thinking of a big beach bonfire."

Breeze got in and the two looked at each other. He pulled on his seatbelt.

Moon put the car in gear. "You serious about the seatbelt?"

235

"You've got yours on. Doesn't it feel good to feel safe?"

Moon gave him a withering look. "You have blood on your breath."

"Better hers than yours. Call it a goodbye gift."

"Better be," Moon snorted.

Breeze leaned across and nuzzled the beauty's pale throat. She placed a soft hand to his smooth cheek.

"You just like my scars," Moon whispered, her fingertips tracing around Breeze's ugly throat scar gifted by Jester.

"The ugliest scars are on the inside."

"Have you seen your neck?" Moon asked. "It's like you tried to shave with a lawnmower."

"You should see Tim's."

The duo laughed as Moon hit the gas and sped into traffic.

"I can run faster than this," Breeze teased.

"You also drink animal blood."

"True. But it's not so bad."

Breeze was practically laughing before the words left his mouth. Drinking blood from anything other than a human was nasty, but it was the price he paid to be alive.

Or rather, to not be dead.

Made in the USA
Monee, IL
18 August 2025

22461974R00134